KU-107-280

THE INVOICE

JONAS KARLSSON

TRANSLATED FROM THE SWEDISH BY NEIL SMITH

HIGHLAND
REGIONAL
LIBRARY

1

WITHDRAWN

ISIS
LARGE
PRINT

First published in Great Britain 2016
by
Hogarth
an imprint of Vintage

First Isis Edition
published 2018
by arrangement with
Vintage
Penguin Random House

The moral right of the author has been asserted

Copyright © 2011 by Jonas Karlsson
Translation © 2016 by Neil Smith
All rights reserved

A catalogue record for this book is available
from the British Library.

ISBN 978–1–78541–511–1 (hb)
ISBN 978–1–78541–517–3 (pb)

Published by
F. A. Thorpe (Publishing)
Anstey, Leicestershire

Set by Words & Graphics Ltd.
Anstey, Leicestershire
Printed and bound in Great Britain by
T. J. International Ltd., Padstow, Cornwall

This book is printed on acid-free paper

3800 18 0005382 3

HIGH LIFE HIGHLAND

THE INVOICE

It's an unremarkable life, I guess, nothing special. I'm in my thirties, I work part time in a video store in Stockholm, most of my friends are busy with their families, I live alone. I suppose you'd say I have an ordinary life . . . But I love this city, and even though my flat is small it suits me, I'm comfo   in through my windows at just the right angle, and I can hear all the sounds of summer life down in the street. And there's a really good ice-cream stall just near my building, which sells my favourite flavours. So, ordinary maybe, but happy. Yes, I think it's fair to say I'm a happy man. And isn't that enough?

SPECIAL MESSAGE TO READERS

THE ULVERSCROFT FOUNDATION
(registered UK charity number 264873)
was established in 1972 to provide funds for
research, diagnosis and treatment of eye diseases.
Examples of major projects funded by
the Ulverscroft Foundation are:-

- The Children's Eye Unit at Moorfields Eye Hospital, London
- The Ulverscroft Children's Eye Unit at Great Ormond Street Hospital for Sick Children
- Funding research into eye diseases and treatment at the Department of Ophthalmology, University of Leicester
- The Ulverscroft Vision Research Group, Institute of Child Health
- Twin operating theatres at the Western Ophthalmic Hospital, London
- The Chair of Ophthalmology at the Royal Australian College of Ophthalmologists

You can help further the work of the Foundation
by making a donation or leaving a legacy.
Every contribution is gratefully received. If you
would like to help support the Foundation or
require further information, please contact:

THE ULVERSCROFT FOUNDATION
The Green, Bradgate Road, Anstey
Leicester LE7 7FU, England
Tel: (0116) 236 4325

website: www.foundation.ulverscroft.com

CHAPTER
ONE

It was such an incredible amount, 5,700,000 kronor. Impossible to take seriously. I assumed it must be one of those fake invoices, the sort you hear about on television and in the papers. Unscrupulous companies trying to defraud people, often the elderly, out of their money.

It was very well done. There was no denying that. The logo looked genuine, at least to me. I don't really know, I don't get much post, apart from the usual bills. This one looked pretty similar. Except for the amount, of course. W. R. D., it said in large letters, and the bit about conditions of payment was very convincing. The whole thing had that dry, factual tone, just like something from a genuine organisation.

But if it was genuine, there must have been a massive mistake. Some computer must have got me mixed up with a big company, or maybe a foreign consortium. 5,700,000 kronor. Who gets bills like that? I chuckled at the thought that someone might actually pay that amount of money by mistake and never question it.

I drank a glass of juice, dropped some advertising leaflets into the recycling box, all those offers and brochures that somehow managed to get past the "No adverts, please" sign, then put on my jacket and went off to work.

I worked part time in a video shop for enthusiasts. There were two of us who took it in turns to stand there two or three days each week, placing orders, sorting films as they came in, cataloguing and putting them on the shelves. Every now and then I was able to help a customer find the right film or explain why a special edition with extra material hadn't come in yet, or possibly didn't include a specific interview that the customer had seen online and which they thought cast the director in question in an entirely new light, and which he or she (usually he) could reproduce pretty much verbatim for me if I felt like listening. Mostly, though, I just stood there thinking about other things.

The walk was a bit windy, but it was the start of light-jacket weather, and most of the trees already had plenty of leaves on their branches. As I walked I thought about the invoice, and wondered how they had managed to get hold of my name and address. Did they just pick the first one they came across? Unless perhaps there was someone else with very similar details?

The windows of the shop were covered by a greenish-yellow layer of pollen, and the door was tricky to open. It didn't seem to matter how we adjusted the closing mechanism. Either the door was hard to shift or it flew open at the slightest touch. Today it stopped halfway.

The floor felt sticky under my feet as I walked to the counter to hang my jacket on the hook beneath it. I put a pot of coffee on to brew in the little kitchen behind the desk. Something had burned onto the bottom of the jug, and Tomas — who worked the other days — said he never drank anything out of it, but I didn't think it was that much of a problem. Quite the opposite, in fact — it gave a bit of a kick to what was otherwise a pretty insipid drink.

I pushed the door of the cupboard under the sink several times because it wouldn't shut properly — it was missing its little magnet-thing. Each time it swung open again a couple of centimetres. In the end I got a bit of sticky tape, rolled it up and stuck it to the inside of the door, and that kept it closed.

Under the counter there was a basket containing the films that had been returned last week, the ones Tomas hadn't bothered to put back on the shelves. I sat there looking at them as I waited for the coffee. There was a Kubrick, a Godard and *The Spanish Prisoner* by David Mamet. I turned the case over and read the back. It had been a long time since I'd watched it. That was when I was still with the love of my life, Sunita, and we would take turns to show each other our favourite films. I'm not even sure if we managed to get to the end of it. She didn't think it was that great.

When the coffee was ready I found a bit of milk in the fridge that was only a couple of days old. I poured some in and drank as I put the rest of the films out.

As I was on my way back to the counter, I felt my shoes sticking to the floor again. I assumed someone must have spilled some Coke or something similar, because wherever I walked my shoes seemed to stick to the lino flooring. It sounded kind of funny, actually. Well, it did if you moved with the right sort of rhythm.

I sat for a while behind the counter and pondered the possibility that someone had stolen my identity — cloned it, or whatever the word was. And had then ordered something and let the company invoice me for that insane amount. But what could you order that cost 5,700,000 kronor? It seemed to me that they ought to have better safeguards in place for this sort of thing.

Sometime between eleven and half past we usually got a brief period of direct sunlight in the shop. I tried leaning over and tilting my head to see if I could work out what was making the floor sticky, and, sure enough, from the right angle you could see little islands of what was probably a spilled soft drink. I stared at it for a while. It looked a bit like a map of the world, if you removed parts of Asia and Australia. I squinted. Africa looked really good. Not to mention what were probably Greenland and Alaska. But, I reasoned, that's probably only because we're not so familiar with the geographic details of those regions. I thought for a while about which countries' shapes I knew best, apart from Sweden, of course, and came to the conclusion that it was probably still the ones in northern Europe. A short while later the sun disappeared over the rooftops. But the stickiness was still there: I could hear it clearly every time I walked across it.

I called Jörgen, my boss, and asked if we could buy a mop. He said that was fine. And that it was probably good to have one for future use, and that it would be nice if I could clean the whole floor.

"Just keep the receipt," he said.

So I went to the hardware shop and bought one of those buckets with a strainer where you can squeeze the water out of the mop that comes with it. I filled it with warm water and realised that I should have bought some sort of floor-cleaner or washing-up liquid, then reasoned that it would probably be okay as long as the water was hot enough. I cleaned every bit of floor in the shop. It looked pretty good. The whole shop felt nicer. Almost a bit luxurious. I changed the water a couple of times, then, finally, mopped the soles of my shoes as well. Then I sat for a while, changing the background on my mobile phone. I switched it off, then on again, and changed the background once more.

Just in time for lunch my friend Roger came in. When I emerged from the toilet he was standing there talking on his phone. He nodded in my direction. Then he disappeared back out into the street. Twenty minutes later he came back in and asked if he could eat the rest of my takeaway. "You don't mind, do you?" he said, and I told him I didn't.

He sat down on the stool behind the counter and slurped up the remaining noodles and meat. He said he'd had a cold for almost three weeks, but that it finally seemed to be on the way out.

"To start with, it was like just a bit of a sore throat," he said as he chewed the food. "Then it turned into a *really* bad sore throat, the sort where it hurts to swallow. Then it went down my tubes and turned into one of those real bastard coughs, the tickly sort where you can't sleep properly. I called the doctor's and said I needed penicillin, but by the time I got there my temperature had gone down and the cough was a bit better. So they refused to give me a prescription. They told me to take paracetamol instead, and come back if it got worse. But it didn't. It just got better."

He tried to cough, but couldn't really manage it. He sighed and shook his head. Then he went on eating until the aluminium tray was scraped clean. Then he pushed it away and asked if we'd had any new films in, then, when I said we hadn't, he sighed again and looked out through the window.

"Well," he said, "I'd better get going."

He grabbed a handful of the sweets we keep to offer children, then disappeared out through the door. I followed him, thinking I might as well hang up the faded red "Open" flag.

No customers came in that afternoon either, so I had a chance to sort some invoices. I added the receipt for the mop and bucket. I punched holes and put everything in folders. Jörgen had a particular way he wanted things organised. Receipts in a green folder and unpaid invoices in a blue one. Then he would pay those himself and transfer them to the green folder.

As I was sitting there leafing through the folders, I found myself thinking once more about the odd invoice I'd received. I noticed that some companies printed the full amount, down to the last öre. That made it look like a very long number. Sometimes it was hard to see the little decimal point between the zeroes. Maybe that's what had happened to me, I thought. Maybe they'd just missed the decimal point, unless perhaps I hadn't noticed it? No, that couldn't be right. Because even if you removed two of the zeroes, it was still an insanely large amount. I certainly hadn't ordered anything that cost 57,000. I'd remember something like that. And what did W. R. D. stand for? I had a bit of a look to see if I could find anything similar among the shop's invoices, but there was nothing like it there. No, I thought. There must have been some sort of mistake somewhere, simple as that.

CHAPTER
TWO

Pretty much exactly a month later a reminder arrived. With a surcharge for late payment. The amount had risen to 5,700,150 kronor. I looked at the sheet of paper more closely. There was no question that it was my name and my address on it. And there was no missing decimal point. There was no doubt about the amount. This time the invoice was from a payment clearance company, SweEx.

We cannot enter into correspondence, it stated clearly in the middle of the page. *All appeals should be directed to our client.* Then a telephone number.

I called the number that was printed at the bottom of the page and found myself listening to an automated voice that welcomed me and said: "Please describe the reason for your call in your own words."

I made an attempt to explain why I was ringing, but before I had finished the automated voice interrupted me and said I would be put through to an operator.

"You are currently number thirty-six in the queue. Waiting time is estimated to be two hours and twenty-five minutes."

When I had been waiting quarter of an hour, the automated voice declared that the waiting time was now estimated to be two hours and forty minutes. I smiled at the absurdity of a waiting time that just kept growing, and seeing as the whole thing was really all a mistake I decided to let them work it out for themselves while I went out and bought myself an ice-cream.

It was a gloriously sunny day. Not a cloud in the sky, and the temperature was approaching thirty degrees in the shade. Down by the kiosk people were crowded into the shadow of the projecting roof, as if taking cover from rain. I stood and waited out in the square for a while, but fairly quickly felt the sun burning my scalp and neck, so I too pushed my way in under the little roof. People were chatting about all sorts of subjects, then suddenly I heard an older woman say to a young man of seventeen or eighteen: "How much was yours?"

I didn't hear his reply, but her reaction was clear enough: "Oh, well, you were lucky, then."

The young man muttered again. It was impossible to make out what he was saying because his mouth was full of ice-cream, and he also had his back to me.

The woman went on: "Yes, but compared to a lot of other people you've got off pretty lightly."

I wondered what they were talking about, but it was difficult to draw any conclusions when I could only hear her side of the conversation. "That's because you haven't been around long enough to get very old yet," the woman suddenly declared. "It's supposed to be worst for people around forty or so."

The young man mumbled something, short and unintelligible.

9

"I know," the woman went on, "because they've just carried on regardless, not expecting this at all. They thought everything was going to last for ever and that the state was going to pay for the whole thing. Imagine! Well, it'll only take you four or five years, then you'll have caught up. But for them . . . well . . ."

She was holding her jacket over one arm, and was facing in my direction as she waited for her son, or grandson, or whatever he was, to finish his ice-cream. The young man went on muttering in a hopelessly low voice. I tried to move closer so I could hear better, but it was practically impossible to make out a single word. "Still a lot of money," I thought it sounded like.

Eventually it was my turn. As usual I went for a small tub with two scoops. Mint chocolate and raspberry. My two favourites.

On my way back up in the lift, I couldn't help overhearing a girl with several different necklaces on as she talked on her phone. She seemed very stressed. She pulled out a big leather-bound diary from her handbag, then leafed through it aimlessly, back and forth, making her necklaces jangle against each other, and even though her hair was tied up she kept brushing a loose strand from her face as she talked.

"Okay, could I borrow half the amount then? . . . No, I realise that . . . Okay, but what about half the amount? . . . Yes. Right. Yes. I've checked with my bank, and they've promised ten, but that's still . . . Yes."

She made a small note in her diary.

"But if I could borrow half the amount from you, then . . . Yes. The invoice comes to —"

10

She caught my eye and suddenly fell silent. As if she had only just noticed that I was standing there. The person at the other end went on talking as the girl murmured in reply.

For some reason these two overheard conversations left me feeling uneasy. It was as though they were talking about something that ought to concern me, something I'd missed. A bit like when you've been away and come back to find everyone talking about a celebrity who's said something funny, or humming an infectious summer hit that everyone else has heard but you've got no idea about.

By the time I got back to my flat there was hardly any ice-cream left. I scraped out the last drips, and managed to spill some on the payment reminder that was still lying there. It struck me that if you don't pay companies like that you end up with a black mark on your credit record — the sort of thing that can be hard to get rid of, even if it later turns out to have been a mistake.

The next time I called the queue was only an hour. But after a while the wait was recalculated once more, and had soon risen to two hours and seven minutes. At one point I got down to half an hour, and at worst it was up at six hours. I switched to speakerphone, put my phone down on the coffee table and left it there as the call went on. I plugged the charger into the wall while I played *Fallout: New Vegas* and listened to the Mahavishnu Orchestra.

Afternoon turned to evening, and evening turned to night, and eventually I slid into my gloomiest mood. A state that could easily last for hours. Sometimes I would put on particularly mournful music, melancholic songs by Jeff Buckley or Bon Iver, preferably some tormented young man singing about his broken heart and crushed dreams, so I could really wallow in pain and sadness. Just sit there and sink deeper into longing and misery. It had its own quite specific feeling of satisfaction. A bit like when you pick at an old wound, a scab — you just can't help it. But after a while I got fed up and dug out a couple of old magazines to reread. I managed to doze off on the sofa in the middle of a long article about projectors and wireless media players.

It was eight o'clock the following morning when I finally got through. A high-pitched, slightly hoarse female voice answered. I started by asking what the hell was wrong with their queuing system.

"It's completely insane," I said. "First it's an hour, then all of a sudden it's twice that. Then it halves again, but before you know it the waiting time's gone up to three hours."

She apologised and said that the system was still under development.

"There are still a few teething problems," she said. "The idea was to develop a more dynamic, customer-centred queuing service. At the moment it takes the length of the current call and adjusts the estimated waiting time from that. But sometimes it can be a little misleading . . ."

12

"No kidding," I said.

"Well," she said, "what can I do for you?"

I said I'd received an invoice, and that there must be some mistake, and would she mind correcting it? She listened carefully, then explained that everything was in order. There was no mistake, and no, I wasn't the first person to call. I said I hadn't ordered anything, or requested any services, but she maintained that the invoice was still correct. When I wondered what this was all about, she sighed and asked if I never read the papers, watched television or listened to the radio? I had to admit that I didn't really keep up with the news.

"Well," she said, and I got the impression that she could have been smiling at the other end of the line. "It's time to pay up now."

CHAPTER
THREE

Small strands of heat clouds were appearing in the sky through the window. It had to be the hottest day of the year so far. It looked like everything out there was quivering. Some children were running about on the pavement below, squirting each other with water-pistols. I could hear their delighted cries when they were hit by the sprays of cool water. On the balcony opposite a woman was shaking a rug. The sound of a spluttering moped echoed off the walls of the buildings. It died away, then came back. It sounded like someone was going from one address to the other, looking for something.

"Have you got Beta or Link?" the woman said on the phone.

"What did you say?" I said.

"Which payment system have you signed up with?"

"No idea," I said. "I don't think I got one at all."

"No?" she said.

"No."

"But you do have a plan?"

"A plan?"

"You've got a payment plan, linked to your E. H. account?"

I waited a moment.

"I don't think so," I said.

"You haven't registered?" she said.

"No," I said. "Should I have?"

She didn't say anything for a while, so I repeated the question.

"Is that something I should have done?"

She cleared her throat.

"Well, let me put it like this: yes."

I felt a sudden urge to sit down.

"But what . . . what am I supposed to be paying for?" I said.

"What?" she said.

"Yes?"

"Everything," she said.

"What do you mean, everything?" I asked.

I was sitting on the floor, with my back against the kitchen wall and my legs pulled up to my chest. The knees of my jeans were starting to look a bit threadbare. It wouldn't be long before I had a hole there, whether I liked it or not. And even though I realised it probably wasn't fashionable any more, I still thought it would look a bit cool.

She hesitated a moment before answering, but even though she was silent, I could hear the weariness in her breathing.

"Where are you calling from?" she asked.

"I'm at home," I said.

"At home. Okay. Look around you. What can you see?"

I raised my eyes from the floor and looked around the room.

"I see my kitchen," I said.

"So, what can you see there?"

"Er . . . the sink. Some dirty dishes . . . A table."

"Look out of the window."

"Okay."

I stood up and went over to the kitchen window, which was open slightly. I'd left it open all night. Maybe a few days. I couldn't remember. The heat had more or less erased the boundary between outside and in. The other day I had a bird in the kitchen for what must have been half an hour. I don't know what sort it was, but it was very pretty. It fluttered to and fro between the kitchen cupboards, then sat on the kitchen table for a while before flying out again.

"What can you see outside?" the woman asked down the phone.

"Buildings," I said. "And a few trees . . ."

"What else?"

"More buildings, and the street, a few cars . . ."

"What else?"

"I can see a blue sky, the sun, a few clouds, people, children playing on the pavement, adults, shops, cafés . . . People out together . . ."

"Exactly. Can you smell anything?"

"Er . . . yes."

I breathed in the smell of the street. It was sweet and warm with summer scents. Flowers, a shrub of some sort? Some old food? A faint smell of something slightly rotten, and petrol. Typical summer smells. Almost a bit Mediterranean. I could hear the moped again now.

"You can feel something, can't you?" the woman continued. "You're feeling feelings, thinking of different things, friends and acquaintances. And I presume you have dreams?"

She was no longer bothering to wait for me to reply.

"What do you mean?" I said.

"Do you dream at night?" she went on.

"Sometimes."

"Hmm. Do you imagine all that is free?"

I didn't say anything for a while.

"Well, I suppose I thought . . ."

"Is that really what you thought?" she said.

I tried to come up with a reply, but my thoughts were going round in circles without formulating themselves into any sort of order. The woman on the phone went on, giving a long explanation of the division of costs, resolutions, single payments and deduction systems. It sounded almost as if she knew it off by heart.

"But how can it amount to so much?" I said, when I could speak again.

"Well," she said, "being alive costs."

I said nothing for a while, because I didn't know what to say.

"But," I eventually said, "I had no idea it was so expensive . . ."

CHAPTER
FOUR

I looked at the payment reminder from the collection company. I ran my finger across the ice-cream stain. I felt foolish. Unmasked, somehow. I felt the same way I used to feel back in school many years ago when the teacher would ask questions designed to reveal how wrong your reasoning was. The children were heading off down the street, they were about to disappear round the corner. The sound of the moped was increasingly distant. A man had arrived on a bike and was busy chaining it to a lamp-post.

"But I've always paid my taxes?" I said.

She laughed. I sank back down onto the floor. Somehow that felt the most comfortable way to sit right now.

"This isn't a tax," she said.

She was silent for a few moments, as if she were expecting me to comment, but I didn't know what to say so she carried on talking of her own accord.

"Tax. That's barely enough to cover day-to-day maintenance. Besides, I presume you don't belong to the group that —"

She stopped again, and I heard her tapping at a keyboard.

"Let's see, what did you say your date of birth and ID number were?"

I told her, and heard her type in the numbers. She drummed her fingers gently against the phone as she waited.

"Right. Let's see, you're . . . thirty-nine years old. Hmm . . . and you haven't made any payments at all?"

"No, I had no idea that —"

She interrupted me mid-sentence. "Well, obviously it's going to amount to a fair sum."

I heard her clicking, as if there were more pages to look through.

"Hmm," she went on, "that's a lot of money."

Several rays of sunlight were falling across the kitchen floor. One of them reached my legs. I stretched my hand carefully back and forth, in and out of the light. Why hadn't anyone said anything? I wondered, and as if the woman at the authority could hear my thoughts, she went on in a rather strict tone of voice: "I'm so fed up of hearing people say they didn't know anything. We've run several online campaigns over the past year, we've had adverts in the papers and handed out information leaflets at schools and workplaces. You'll have to be a bit more observant in the staffroom or canteen next time."

"The staffroom?"

"Yes, that's usually where the notices get put up. About things like this."

"But," I said, pulling my hand out of the light, "there's absolutely no way I can pay."

She was completely quiet for a while.

"No?"

I considered the meagre income from my part-time job in the video shop. The little that was left over from my wages, which were paid partly cash in hand, plus a small inheritance that was gradually shrinking, made up the sum total of my savings.

On the other hand, I'd never had any particularly large expenses. My flat was small and old-fashioned, and the rent was low. I had no one but myself to support, and I didn't have a lavish lifestyle. A few computer games every now and then, music, a bit of food, hardly any phone bill to speak of, and I got films free from the shop. Sometimes I would pay for a beer or lunch for Roger, but that didn't happen often these days. I always imagined I was free of extra financial responsibilities of that sort. Other people had careers and acquired houses and families and children. Got married, divorced, started their own businesses and set up limited companies. Employed accountants, bought property, leased cars, borrowed money. I was pretty happy on my own, without a big social circle, or anyone to cause any problems.

"It's completely impossible," I said. "At most, I've got about forty thousand in the bank."

"What about your flat?" she said.

"Rented."

She said nothing for a moment. Then she said abruptly: "Hold on a moment and I'll check . . ."

She put the phone down and I heard her walk away. In the background there was the sound of keyboards being tapped, other people who seemed to be talking on the phone. A couple of telephones ringing. She was gone for some time. Eventually I heard her come back and pick up the phone again.

"Do you own anything of value?"

"Er, no . . . the television, maybe."

"Hmm," she said, "television sets aren't worth anything these days. Is it big?"

"Thirty-two inches, maybe."

"Forget it. That's nothing. No car?"

"No."

"I see," she said, and sighed. "You'll have to pay what you can. Then we'll start with an inventory of your home and see what that comes up with. That will give us an idea of what level of debt we're going to end up at . . ."

"And what happens then?"

"That depends entirely on the amount."

"In what way?"

"Well, we do have a debt ceiling."

"What does that mean?"

"That means we can only permit debts up to a certain limit . . . I mean, in order to maintain continued access . . ."

"To what?"

"To . . . everything."

"Are you going to kill me?"

She laughed. It was evidently a stupid question and I felt rather relieved at her reaction.

"No," she said, "we aren't going to kill you. But I'm sure you can appreciate that you can't carry on enjoying experiences if you don't have the means to pay for them?"

I held my hand out towards the shaft of light again and felt the heat of the sun. There really was a big difference in temperature, even though it was actually only a matter of a few centimetres. The woman at the other end of the line interrupted my thoughts.

"What on earth have you been thinking? All these years? Hasn't it ever occurred to you that you should be paying your way?"

"Well, I didn't actually know that we had to pay. Why —?"

She interrupted me again. She had obviously heard all this before. She knew it wasn't going to lead anywhere. She'd run out of patience for excuses and explanations. I could hear voices in the background, and got the impression that my time was running out.

"Let me put it like this: have you ever been in love?"

"Er, yes."

"When?"

"A few times, I suppose."

"More than once, then?"

"Yes. I mean, well, once properly."

She was running on autopilot. Probably already thinking about the next conversation. But she still sounded friendly, in a professional way. "There, you see, you must have experienced some wonderful things."

I thought about Sunita, who I had been with for several years back in the nineties. A small wave of memories coursed through my body. A pang of melancholy.

"Yes, I suppose so," I said.

She was obviously in a hurry to hang up now, there was no mistaking it. As if she had suddenly realised that we had exceeded our allotted time. As if it had struck her that she didn't have time to make idle conversation with me.

"Well, if there's nothing else, thank you for calling."

"Hang on a moment," I said. "How do I . . .? What can I do?"

She must have loads of calls waiting.

Maybe she could see the constantly rising number of people in the queue. She probably had a boss who was eager for her to move on. She was talking faster now.

"Have you checked with your bank?"

"No, but . . . It doesn't really seem very likely that I . . ."

"No, I suppose not."

She sighed audibly, and someone said something in the office where she was sitting.

"Do you know what?" she said. "Take a thorough look at your finances in peace and quiet — people usually manage to come up with something — and then call me again."

"But," I said, "the queue to get through is really long . . ."

"You can have my direct number."

"Okay."

I got her number and wrote it on the bottom of the ice-cream tub.

"My name's Maud," she said.

We hung up and I sat there for a long time with the phone in my hand. The sun had passed behind a cloud. The warm ray of light across my knees was no longer there.

CHAPTER
FIVE

I could hear ringing in my ears. The sort of sound you get after a concert or a sinus infection. I'm not sure when it started. Maybe it was just that long phone call. It was already as hot as Greece inside the flat. And I knew it was only going to get hotter when the sun moved completely round to this side of the building later in the afternoon. I wondered if it was best to carry on leaving the windows open, or if I was only letting in more heat. An overwhelming feeling of tiredness washed over me. I hauled myself up on to the sofa, thinking that somewhere at the back of my mind I'd always had an inkling about this. The feeling that life couldn't really be this simple.

I leaned back, took some deep breaths and felt a weak breeze just about reach me as I sat there on the sofa. I surrendered to the heavy, numbing tiredness and felt myself slowly drift from consciousness and into a wonderful drowsiness where time and space and thought gradually dissolved. After a while I fell asleep, and only woke up when my phone buzzed.

It was a text from Roger. *Call me*, it said. But I didn't feel like calling. Not just then.

I stretched out my legs and lay back on the sofa. The fabric was warm. I felt warm, right down to the roots of my hair. Everything was warm. For a brief moment I got the impression that everything was just a dream, until I caught sight of the ice-cream tub and the number written on the bottom. All of a sudden it felt pretty irresponsible that I'd gone out to buy ice-cream when my financial situation was so precarious.

I had a bit of a headache when I stood up and wandered aimlessly round the flat until I finally ended up in front of my collection of vinyl records. What could they be worth? There were quite a few genuine collector's items. I had a number of limited-edition Blu-ray films, and then there were my instruments, of course, but no matter how I tried I couldn't get anywhere close to the amount required. 5,700,150 kronor was more money than I could even imagine.

I toyed with the idea of simply running away. Leaving the country. How many resources would they devote to tracking down someone like me?

I could take the bus to Nynäshamn, then the ferry to Gotland, and hide out there on some pebbly beach. Or get the train to Copenhagen, then hitchhike down to Germany . . . What then, though? I could get all my money out of the bank, buy a plane ticket to the USA, and stroll about Manhattan drinking milkshakes and eating pastrami sandwiches. In a way, the thought of just taking off like that was quite tempting. But what would I do once I'd actually got there? And the thought of never coming back . . . No, I was happy here, after all. I had my friends here. All my memories. I liked my flat, the changing seasons. I liked lying on the sofa . . . But of course if there was no other option . . .

I picked up my phone and held it in my hand for a while. If Mum was still alive I would have called her. That would have cheered her up, something as simple as that, even if she'd have been worried about the size of the debt. Maybe she'd have been able to come up with a solution. She usually could. I stood for a while tossing my phone from hand to hand. In the end I rang the only number I could think of.

CHAPTER
SIX

Maud answered on the second ring. She sounded much calmer now. It felt odd, after the long wait in the queue the previous evening, suddenly to get through to her straight away this time. It made me feel a bit special.

"What would you do if I just disappeared?" I asked.

"Disappeared?" she said.

"Yes."

"In principle it doesn't really matter where you are. This applies to everyone. Top-up payments, or in your case the whole amount, can be made from anywhere. And in whatever currency you choose. You can live wherever you like, as long as you don't try to avoid your duty to pay."

I thought for a moment.

"And if I did, what then?"

"Well," she said, "we'd put out an alert for you. Your bank accounts, driving licence, passport, credit cards would all be frozen or revoked. You'd be a marked man. You'd never be able to get a loan, for instance. It would be — how can I put it? — difficult. Why, are you thinking about it?"

"No," I said, and sighed. "I don't think I am."

"Good," Maud said, "because I'm under orders to report any suspicions about potential absconders. It would be nice not to have to do that."

I thought I could detect a hint of a west-coast accent, and tried to work out where she was from. She was doing her best to speak a sort of standard Swedish, but every now and then a trace of a chirpy, rounded intonation crept into the end of her sentences. It sounded rather cute, somehow.

"So how are you getting on with the money?" she said.

I rubbed my face and tried to sound like I was on the case. Like I'd done nothing but play with numbers and call people for help since we last spoke.

"Not great," I said.

"You don't have any investments or shares?"

"No."

"Jewellery? Gold?"

"I've got a few rings, that's all . . . a couple of candlesticks. But that doesn't . . ."

I sat down on the sofa and was about to lie back again when it occurred to me that she'd probably be able to tell from my voice that I was lying down. That wouldn't make a very good impression.

"Can't I just work off the debt, bit by bit?" I said.

Maud took a deep breath. Once again I had the feeling that this wasn't the first time she'd had to explain this. She sounded rather mechanical when she replied.

"Assuming that you have a normal capacity to work, naturally we'll conduct an evaluation of your abilities, relative to the amount owing. But there are a lot of people to be investigated and of course that involves a great deal of administration — it's not at all certain that will even be necessary. And, as I said before, we do have a debt ceiling, and once that's been exceeded there's no way we can grant continued access."

"What's the debt ceiling?"

"It's calculated according to a formula that takes account of age, place of residence, particular experiences, success, proximity to the sea. That sort of thing. Quality of home and relationships, et cetera. Taken as a whole, that constitutes your personal quantity of Experienced Happiness. Your levels will be constantly updated, provided that all information can be verified. It's all officially administered, of course, but I'm afraid I can't make an estimate as things stand . . . Have you had any notable setbacks?"

I stared at a small mark on the wall opposite the sofa. It had been there for as long as I could remember, and I rather liked it. It felt reassuring. Homely. I wondered if it had been made by me or the previous tenant.

"How do you mean?"

"Okay, let me start with this," she went on. "Are you disabled?"

"No," I said.

"Do you suffer from any illnesses?"

"No. Well, nothing . . . no. I get a bit of asthma sometimes."

"Asthma?"

"Yes, a bit. Occasionally, in the spring."

"Oh?"

"And I might be a bit lactose intolerant."

"Hmm, that isn't applicable. Not any more. Not now there are so many new products and alternatives available . . . Did you grow up with both your parents?"

"Yes."

"There you go. Yes, that marks it up . . ."

Images from my childhood drifted through my head. Mum smoking a Blend cigarette under the extractor fan in the kitchen, Dad bent over the car with the bonnet up, my little tricycle, the broken doorbell. Long grass at the back of the house and the rusty lawnmower that was supposed to cut it.

"But we weren't especially rich or anything . . ." I said.

"That doesn't make any difference to the experience, does it?"

"I don't know, I think maybe it does . . ."

"How do you mean, exactly?"

"Well, if I'd been brought up . . . I mean, it was pretty tough sometimes when Dad was the only one working . . ."

"But you were happy?"

"What?"

"Was your childhood satisfactory?"

I hesitated for a few seconds.

"Well, yes, I'd have to say it was . . ."

"There, you see?"

I wondered how old she was. She sounded a bit older than me, but that didn't necessarily mean that she really was. The slight hoarseness in her voice lent her a certain veiled charm, but she could have been five, ten years younger than me. That sort of thing is always hard to work out. Maybe it was just her official tone, that way of reciting things quickly, or the fact that she knew things that I didn't. It wouldn't be the first time. I often felt about seventeen years old mentally. And she was definitely older than that, no matter what.

"Like you replied to our questionnaires . . ." she went on. I closed my eyes and tried to focus my thoughts in the heat.

"Hang on a moment," I said. "Questionnaires?"

"Yes, you indicated . . . let's see . . ."

I sat up a bit straighter on the sofa. I had little beads of sweat on my forehead and temples. I could feel the phone getting damp and slippery against my cheek.

"What questionnaires?" I said.

"Our inquiries show that . . ."

She paused, and I heard her click to open something on her computer. Now I remembered some questionnaires and forms I'd filled in several months ago. Big things, with all sorts of different questions and boxes you had to tick. I think I did them while I was on the toilet. Then you just had to stick them in the pre-paid envelope and put them in the post.

"I'm getting several results here . . . Let's see . . ."

I stood up and started to walk round the room.

"Yes, but . . ." I said. "I thought filling those in was just a bit of fun . . . I didn't really take it seriously."

"You didn't?"

"No, because then I'd have thought about it a bit more . . ."

"You didn't really think about it?"

32

"Well, not really . . ."

"Here we are . . . Five written surveys and one telephone poll."

I suddenly remembered a phone call, something like six months ago. A young woman. I enjoyed talking to her. She had a sexy voice, and for once she wasn't trying to sell anything. It was kind of fun, choosing between the possible answers: agree strongly, agree, disagree or don't know.

Maud went on: "I'm getting quite a high reading from this."

I wandered into the kitchen, then back into the living room.

"Really?" I said. "Oh . . . I must have been happy that day."

"But you did answer truthfully?"

"That depends how you look at it."

"What do you mean?"

I walked up and down between the sofa and the wall, glad Maud couldn't see me.

"It changes," I said. "From day to day. I mean, sometimes you're in a good mood, so things don't feel so important . . ."

"Really?"

I sat down on the sofa, but stood up again immediately.

"I think it's rather unprofessional to base everything on surveys like that. I mean, how was I to know that my answers would form the basis of —"

She interrupted me again.

"Obviously that's not the whole picture. Your responses are only advisory. The calculations are ninety per cent based on absolute facts. But all the evidence suggests that self-evaluation gives a fairly good prognosis."

I tried to remember those questions, and what I had answered. Maybe I'd been trying to make out I was more successful than I really was? After all, I did like the woman's voice. Maybe I was trying to impress her? I could even have just been messing about and making things up.

"Have you got my answers there?" I said. "What did I say?"

"I've got a general overview. Basically just the scores. I can see the analysis of your results, which are the raw data presented in a more accessible format. If you want more information I'd have to put in a request for your file to be brought up. It could take a while."

I told her I did want more information. She said she'd get back to me and we hung up.

CHAPTER
SEVEN

It was late afternoon before she called back. I could tell that I should have eaten something, even if I wasn't exactly hungry. It was completely still outside, extremely hot, and somewhere in the distance a car alarm was going off.

"There's rather a lot of material," she said. "It's not available digitally yet, and I've only just received it, so obviously I haven't had time to get to grips with the details properly . . ."

"Okay," I said.

I could hear her leafing through some papers. She almost groaned as she picked up something heavy. We exchanged some polite jokes about "the paperless society".

"You wanted the questionnaire results . . ." she eventually said.

"That's right," I said.

"If you could just confirm your address, I can send them to —"

"Have you got them there?" I asked.

"Yes," she said.

"Can't you just tell me what I said?" I went on.

She hesitated for a moment.

"It will take a while to dig them out."

"I can wait," I said.

"Er . . . well, we don't usually . . . over the phone. But if you tell me your address I can send you a copy . . ."

"But," I said, "can't you just read them out? I mean, I've given you my ID number and everything."

She said nothing for a few moments.

"Well, I suppose so," she said slowly.

"Just a few of them," I said.

I heard her shuffling the documents again.

"Okay, you'll have to wait a moment while I go through the file."

"I'm happy to wait," I said.

We sat there like that for two or three minutes without saying much at all. Just the sound of her breathing as she searched through the documents. I found myself thinking that she should put the phone down, then realised that she was probably wearing a headset. She cleared her throat and went on.

"So, what do you want to know, then?" she said.

"Just the first few questions . . ."

"Okay," she said after a brief pause. "Question number one, then . . . let's see . . . age, gender, education . . . But I suppose what you really want to . . . okay, here it is: Do you think your life has a purpose, a meaning? And you answered . . ."

I imagined I could hear her running her finger across the page to the column of answers.

"Yes," she continued. "The first option, in fact. 'Agree strongly'."

Yes, that was true. I had a clear memory now of having given that answer. I wondered if I might have replied with the first option to almost all the questions. I mean, it felt a bit cool to stick to the same response. Sort of like shrugging my shoulders at the questions. Not taking it too seriously.

Maud moved on to the second question.

"Do you feel that your opinions and ideas are listened to at your place of work?"

What opinions and ideas?! I could hardly have any ideas, apart from renting films to people who came into the shop. Maybe sell the odd bag of crisps or two-litre bottle of drink. Jörgen didn't give a damn about any opinions I might have. We never talked about that sort of thing. I got paid, and I kept the shelves tidy. That was all. What was I supposed to answer? Most of the time I just stood there thinking about other things, trying to keep an eye on the time and when I could go home. Sometimes Roger would pop in, and if I had time I'd stand there chatting to him. Maybe check out a few videos on YouTube. I thought it worked pretty well, and I certainly didn't have any better suggestions about how to run things.

Maud was about to read out the third question, but all of a sudden I felt I didn't want to hear any more, and said I had to go. I don't even know if I said goodbye properly.

CHAPTER
EIGHT

With some reluctance, I had to admit that I was actually pretty happy with my life. I didn't really have anything to complain about. No impoverished childhood, no addictions or abuse or emotionally cold upper-class teenage years at a prison-like boarding school. The years I spent in our little terraced house on Fågelvägen seemed to have passed without any real conscious thought. My parents were dead now, but, to be fair, they were both well over seventy when they died, so not even that could be counted as particularly traumatic. And I still had my sister, even though we didn't see much of each other these days. The best thing about her was her kids. In limited doses. I was undeservedly happy with my tranquil existence here in my flat, and I'd never really dreamed of anything more. I hadn't had a proper relationship since Sunita, and naturally I sometimes wished I had a girlfriend, but I had to admit that most of the time I was happy on my own, and the internet came in very useful.

I didn't miss company. On the contrary, I was happy if I could avoid it. Especially compared to my sister's chaotic life, trying to juggle work and preschool and vomiting bugs and family therapy sessions. I couldn't really think of any injustice that had left any deep scars. Roger was always falling out with people. He often told me about the quarrels he had with his brother, or the National Insurance people, the Tax Office, people he owed money to, or who owed him money. Obviously I got upset and miserable sometimes, but most of the time I soon forgot about it and moved on. That sort of thing never really made much of an impression on me. I loved my parents, and of course I missed them, but I didn't actually have a problem accepting the fact that they were gone. That was just the way it was.

I tried to remember the last time I was properly angry. The previous week I swore out loud to myself when the handle of a paper bag broke and all my shopping fell out onto the pavement. I had to carry it all in my arms, and was seriously cross by the time I eventually made it back to the flat. But it passed, and I was soon in a good mood again when I realised I had three copies of the *Metro* in the flat with their crosswords still unsolved.

Maybe I didn't take problems seriously enough, and just took everything that was thrown at me without protest. Was I too gullible, too accepting? Should I set higher demands? Would I actually be better off if I was more suspicious, a better negotiator?

CHAPTER
NINE

I heated up a slice of pizza in the microwave. It was good, but there wasn't enough of it. Then I sat at the kitchen table for a while, just thinking. The soft, warm summer air had become sticky and suffocating. It was difficult to think clearly, all my thoughts just bounced around. Any sense of true harmony was impossible to achieve. I noticed I was having trouble sitting still. So I phoned again. Even though it had gone eight o'clock in the evening.

"I've actually been very anxious," I said.

"You have?" Maud said. "When?"

I pushed my knife and fork together on the plate and suddenly realised I was thirsty. I should have had a drink before I called. I could feel my mouth sticking together with nerves.

"What?" I said. "How do you mean . . .?"

"What days?"

I gulped a few times.

"You mean I'm supposed to remember exactly what days —" She interrupted me without apologising. She was fed up of me now. I could tell.

"If you want a deduction for anxiety, I need to know the precise times."

"I can get a deduction for anxiety?"

"Provided it can be verified, or you can give us specific dates that can be compared with other activities that aren't incompatible with mental ill-health, then obviously you can set reduced mental well-being against your total E. H. score. What year are we talking about?"

I nudged the cutlery round the edge of the plate, a bit like the hands of a clock, and did a quick calculation in my head.

"Er . . . this year," I said.

"Month?"

I wasn't used to lying or making things up. My mouth felt even drier, and I got the impression it was audible in my voice. But on some level I felt I had to make the most of any opportunity, and took a chance.

"January," I said.

"Okay, I can't see any note to that effect," she said.

"No, but it's true."

"Mmm . . . and on a scale of one to five, where one is normal and five incapable of any activity at all?"

"Well, er . . . five," I said.

I thought it was probably best to exaggerate.

"Goodness," she said. "What date?"

"The first."

"The first of January?"

"Mmm. And the second and third."

"Okay. Any other dates?"

I hesitated for a moment.

"No, that was about it . . ." I said.

"So everything was okay again on the fourth?"

"Yes, I suppose so . . ."

"Suddenly nothing?"

"Er . . . yes."

I heard her take a sip of coffee or tea. A drink would have been nice.

"Is this really true?" she said after a brief pause.

I was a hopeless liar. I knew it. It would have been embarrassing to go on.

"Well . . . no," I said.

"No," she said. "I guessed as much. How about you and I agree to stop messing about now? Then we can try to come up with a proper solution to this instead."

"Okay," I said, feeling pathetic. "Sorry."

She murmured something. And I got the impression that she didn't think it was that big an issue. That she was prepared to overlook it, and that she'd probably experienced similar things before.

"But I do suffer from anxiety," I said. "Honestly. I can't remember any specific dates or exactly how bad it was, but . . . well . . . I feel really bad sometimes."

"Okay . . ."

There was a different tone to her voice now. Sympathetic, somehow. A bit like a psychologist, maybe. Perhaps they were trained to sound that way, to keep people calm.

"I often get anxious about nothing special," I said.

"Oh?"

"And I don't know why. I get hurt easily, and I'm very sensitive about everything, without any particular reason. In the spring, for instance, when you'd expect to be happy and cheerful. I often feel a bit depressed then."

I could hear her drinking more coffee as I talked.

"You realise that's all part of the experience, don't you?" she said eventually.

"Sorry?"

"And that it's the whole experience that you're paying for?"

I pulled my fork across the plate, knocking the knife off. It clattered against the porcelain. She went on: "Think about it like this: when you go to the cinema — one day you might see a comedy, the next a tear-jerker. The experience isn't any the less valid as a result. It all gives E. H. points, you see. You know as well as I do that pain isn't a universally negative emotion, don't you?"

I said nothing.

"We wouldn't want to eat nothing but sweet things . . . just as little as we'd want to avoid all adversity. In fact, there has to be a degree of adversity for us to appreciate our blessings. I mean, think about the mix of ingredients in really good food dishes. Like that song Lasse Berghagen sings about Stockholm, 'A mixture of sweet and salt' . . ."

I pushed the plate across the table. Raised my hand and massaged my forehead. She went on: "Well, there's nothing I can do about it now. Your case has already been assessed."

"Is this a punishment?" I said suddenly. "Because I haven't mourned my parents enough?"

"What?" she said, sounding genuinely surprised. "What makes you say that?"

I sighed and pinched the bridge of my nose between my fingers. I could feel myself getting a headache.

"Well, maybe it hasn't had time to sink in properly yet. I've just been carrying on as normal. Is that insensitive of me? I mean . . . maybe I haven't been as upset as I should have been . . . My sister did a lot of crying and screaming, then got all quiet and depressed and all that, but I . . ."

"Don't be daft," she said gently. "This is nothing personal. Your score is entirely experience-based."

"Can I appeal against it?" I said.

"Of course. But that can take a long time, and it doesn't alter things as they stand right now. You see, this is more than a national issue. It's a question of the division of resources. Obviously each country pays a large portion of its total with a collective national amount. But then the bill has to be divided. Between everyone. I'm sure you can understand that. Floods, famine, starvation . . . If you compare that with — what did you say? — feeling a bit miserable in the spring?"

"Mmm," I said. I didn't feel like thinking about it any more for the moment.

After agreeing that I would start by paying what little I had in the bank, we hung up and I realised that I was still very hungry. It occurred to me that I hadn't eaten anything all day apart from that slice of pizza. I went and made a cheese sandwich. I poured myself a glass of full-fat milk, and downed it in one. As soon as I'd

44

finished the first sandwich I immediately made myself another one. I felt insatiable. It was a wonderful feeling to be able to surrender to hunger, instantly, without restraint. The taste of the cheese, bread and milk married to form a wonderful union. Just then I couldn't think of anything nicer.

I sat back down at the kitchen table and realised that all was lost. There was no way to change the situation. I simply had to accept the facts. So what was likely to happen?

As I had already been told, they couldn't kill me. She'd said as much. Through the open window I could hear the birds' evening song. People laughing and talking to each other. Friendly voices. It was approaching the time of day when the whole city relaxed. The sound of voices and footsteps outside kept growing. People going to the pub, sitting at pavement bars. This whole situation no longer felt so important. In a way, the feeling of acceptance that was spreading through me was actually pretty good, relaxing. I made up my mind to drink the rest of the carton of milk. It tasted good, almost all the way to the end.

CHAPTER
TEN

It was late in the evening, but I still called. I'd remained seated at the kitchen table pretty much the whole time, listening to the city outside. I had watched darkness slowly settle over the rooftops as the sounds changed. A couple were arguing. I could hear fragments of what they were saying, but not enough to understand what it was about. A woman laughed loudly, for a long time. A dog barked, and a group of young men sang some football chant. Every so often a gust of cooler air would push its way into the warm kitchen, caressing my face and arms. I sat where I sat, and there was no reason to go anywhere else. Life was just so good, somehow. It was perfectly natural that it should be expensive.

I dialled the number but there was no answer, and it struck me that even Maud must need a break, maybe to go to the loo or get something to eat. Maybe she too was sitting listening to the sounds of the city? Maybe they had a roof terrace? Maybe she was sitting up there smoking a cigarette or drinking a cup of coffee in the balmy summer night? I hung up, waited half an hour, then called again.

"Yes?" Maud said, and sighed. I could clearly hear the irritation in her voice. She knew it was me. She probably had one of those screens where she could see what number was calling. This can't have been what she expected when she gave me her direct number.

"Well, I'm sitting here in the kitchen, experiencing happiness," I said pointedly.

"How nice for you," she said.

"Yes," I said. "I can't help wondering what's going to happen with that?"

She didn't reply immediately.

"How do you mean?" she said.

"I mean, right now I feel really good, and that, along with all the coming experiences — I don't really like to admit it, but . . . well, it's going to happen again. This year, maybe next . . . What's to say that I won't owe five million all over again in a year's time?"

Through the window I could see a drooping pot plant that my neighbour had left out on the balcony when he went away for the summer. Maybe he thought it would survive on nothing but rainwater, but it was unlikely to last much longer in this sort of heat.

Maud let out a deep sigh. She was tired of me now.

"You really don't get it, do you?" she said.

I got no further than a drawn-out vowel, it might have been an "e", and was just about to reply that maybe I didn't get it when she went on regardless: "This is a one-off amount. That's the whole point of it. This is when it's happening."

"What is?" I said. She sighed again.

"Surely you can't have missed . . . This is when we're going to regulate . . . implement the big adjustment. It was made perfectly clear in all the information leaflets. If you have a look through your inbox . . . I think I may even have mentioned it myself . . ."

"But," I interrupted, "it could end up being incredibly unfair. Let's say I'm one of the people paying most now, but then I go and get some disease tomorrow that might torment me for ten, twenty years."

"Of course," Maud said. "But the money has to be paid now. And the past is the only thing we know anything about, isn't it? The future's . . . well, we've got no idea, have we . . .? Neither you nor I can know if we'll still be standing here tomorrow."

We were both silent for a while as we thought about that. I watched a fly struggling against the windowpane, constantly bouncing off it. In the end I said: "I'm sitting down. Aren't you?"

I thought I could almost detect a smile.

"No, I'm not, actually," she said. "I'm standing."

"Have you got one of those adjustable . . .?"

"Precisely. After all, I have to spend a lot of hours on the phone."

I suddenly felt rather sorry for her. It must be an incredibly wearing task, sitting there day after day, dealing with all sorts of agitated people and explaining something that you hadn't yourself come up with. In this sort of heat. Didn't she ever long to be outside? It was actually pretty fantastic that she was prepared to give me so much of her time. How many people could there be in the queue at that moment, waiting to get through? Perhaps she did like me a bit after all?

"What are you wearing?" I said.

It just came out. I hadn't planned to say it. It was as if my brain had gone soft in the heat. As if the whole atmosphere had changed just because it was night. Everything felt a bit unreal. I regretted saying it before I'd even finished the sentence.

"Sorry?" she said, as if she genuinely hadn't heard.

"Nothing," I said quickly. "Sorry. It was nothing."

"Okay," she said, sounding distant again. As if she didn't quite know how to behave when the conversation strayed outside the usual boundaries.

I could feel myself blushing, and it struck me how little it took for me to become keen on a woman. It really didn't take much at all. As long as she wasn't directly off-putting. Often all she had to do was be kind and pleasant. Or not even that. The unpleasant sort could also arouse my curiosity. Most of the time it was enough for a woman to show any sort of interest in me. But not even that was a necessity. I appreciated disinterest as well. In fact, I was even attracted by it. I realised that I didn't actually need anything at all to get my attention. It would probably be easy to trick me into anything at all, as long as it was done with a bit of imagination. I basically thought the best of people, and assumed that most people wished me well. And no matter what the reason, it did feel rather intimate, talking to someone at this time of day. Almost a bit exclusive. What sort of working hours could they have? In fact, wasn't it extremely peculiar that you could call pretty much anytime, and still talk directly to this woman?

I stood up and started looking for the invoice. What sort of official body was W. R. D., anyway? What did it stand for? It sounded made-up. Did it really exist? Didn't the font that the payment demand was printed in look a bit odd? There was actually something rather amateurish about the whole form.

I tried to remember what she'd said. And the more I thought about it, the more it sounded like a classic scam. A young woman with a seductive voice tells a man he owes a load of money, and has to pay it into a particular account. How many films had I seen on that theme? And wasn't three something a bit suspicious about the fact that she was devoting so much time to me? When did she look after the others? And where was she, anyway? Was she even in the same country as me? It was naïve of me not to have thought about all those gangs that operated through numerous ingenious connections and encryption systems and were almost impossible to trace. And this was exactly how they operated. What had I actually heard? Office noises. That could be anything. Maybe even a recording?

I walked about trying to find the invoice, holding the phone to my ear, but with neither Maud nor I saying anything for a long while. Why was she suddenly not speaking? Had she guessed that I suspected something? Maybe I ought to call Roger or my sister and check with one of them? After all, no one I knew had said anything about this. And there was something a bit odd about those people discussing it out in the city, wasn't there? Something not quite right, in an indefinable way. That mother and son talking as if they were reciting a script. And the way she was looking in my direction the whole time. Or the woman in the lift, jangling her necklaces and talking about her invoice and loan a bit *too* explicitly for it to feel natural . . . Obviously they'd been told to get close to me and say those things within earshot.

I closed my eyes and tried to think. It would be ridiculously *foolish* to pay a load of money into an account without checking things out more closely. The more I thought about it, the more incredible it seemed that I would never have heard anything about this before that invoice popped through my letterbox. Maybe they specifically targeted single people with a shaky grasp of what was going on in the world, and got them to believe a load of lies?

When I failed to find the sheet of paper and neither of us had said anything for almost a minute, I went and stood by the window. A shiver of belated insight ran through my body. That was my first reaction, I thought. That was the first thing I thought: Fake invoice. I tried to remember how much information I had given away, apart from my address, date of birth and ID number.

In the end, I said straight out: "How do I know you're not trying to trick me?"

She remained silent. I went on without waiting for her to answer.

"Maybe this is all just a trap? It's the sort of thing you hear about, after all. Have you seen *The Spanish*

Prisoner by David Mamet? That conspiracy film, where everything turns out to have been fake? Or that other one, what's it called? *The Game*, with Michael Douglas. How do I know you're not trying to deceive me, and are going to vanish with all my money?"

She didn't say anything. I thought it felt like a nervous silence. The silence of someone who had been found out. What can anyone say, once everything has been uncovered and revealed?

I couldn't deny that it was incredibly well done. Grandiose, really. Putting together such an advanced plan, appealing to the victim's guilty conscience like that, and making it sound almost plausible. In a way it actually felt a bit unkind to have to put a stop to it. I mean, I'd started to enjoy those conversations. I'd have been happy to carry on talking to her each evening. She was drinking coffee again now. Rustling papers, or tidying something in the office.

"Well," she said eventually, "naturally you're entitled to book a meeting and come up and talk to one of our advisors, if you'd rather do it that way."

CHAPTER
ELEVEN

W. R. D.'s Swedish headquarters consisted of a number of adjoining buildings made of speckled grey granite. An apparently endless flow of people moved to and fro across the shiny stone floor of the main entrance. A large black sign bearing the words "World Resources Distribution" in gold hung above a row of no fewer than six lifts. Along one wall water trickled down smooth, polished granite in a steady, even stream. The large, south-facing glass wall let in plenty of light, and there were big square pots containing what might have been fig trees at the foot of it. There may have been gentle music playing in there, unless it was just the well-judged design itself that was contributing to the harmonious soundscape. Between the third and fourth lifts was a map of the entire complex, with a large "you are here" arrow to indicate where I was.

The advisors were on the eleventh floor, and their reception area had glass doors facing all directions, making it impossible to ignore the view. Straight ahead, opposite the lift, a woman was sitting at a desk looking through some papers and answering the phone. She asked me to take a seat. I sat down in one of the armchairs grouped to one side of her. To my left was an empty conference room, and to the right the sort of open-plan office I imagined Maud worked in. I amused myself by trying to work out which one she might be. There were a dozen or so people in there, and most of them were indeed standing at height-adjustable desks. My attention was taken by a woman with long hair in a brownish-beige dress. She looked calm even though you could see she was talking very quickly. It was surprisingly quiet out where I was sitting, considering the level of activity behind the glass doors. Only one door had frosted glass, and through it came a man with combed-over hair. He introduced himself as Georg and asked me to go with him to one of the meeting rooms.

Georg was wearing a suit with no tie, and looked like he was the same age as me, possibly a few years older. He had thinning dark brown hair with a hint of red in it, and I wondered if he dyed it. He sat down opposite me and put a thick folder on the table.

"Well," he said, looking at me. "You wanted a meeting in person?"

"Er, yes," I said. "I've got a few questions."

He nodded and smiled.

"Hmm," he said. "What sort of questions?"

I held out my hands.

"How it can come to so much, for instance?"

He nodded again. He was clearly used to questions of this sort.

"Let's see, now," he said, opening the folder. "You've been talking to . . ."

"Maud," I said.

He glanced up at me, then looked back down at the folder. He adjusted a long strand of hair that had fallen across his forehead, and ran his finger along the bottom of one page.

"Maud . . . Maud Andersson — yes, that's right. One moment."

He went out to the young woman in reception, then came back in. He sat down and leafed through the file, apparently not bothered by my presence. He had a large pile of documents from the local council, the regional council, schools, the address register, betting companies, and so on. There was a humming sound from the ceiling, from the air conditioning or some sort of ventilation system. I noticed that there were small surveillance cameras in each corner. Simple, flat lenses, big enough to make you realise that it was no secret that every nook and cranny of the room was covered. We were probably being watched the whole time by someone sitting somewhere else. Maybe they were listening in as well.

Through the glass walls, I eventually saw a tall, thin woman in a navy blue jacket and skirt walking between the tables. She had full lips, fair hair cut into the nape of her neck, but longer at the front to form a little arc round her cheeks. She went out into the reception area, then came over towards us, tapped on the glass and pushed the door open when Georg indicated that she could come in.

"Hello," she said to me, holding out her hand.

I stood up and was about to utter the phrase I'd thought out in advance: that she looked just like she sounded on the phone, when I realised that she didn't sound the same at all. I looked at the eyes and hair, and those lips that seemed too full to be entirely natural. And while I was thinking that she didn't look at all like I'd imagined, she introduced herself with a long, complicated surname that I didn't quite catch. It sounded like the name of a bank to me. Or a firm of solicitors. I can't remember what it was, neither her first nor last name. Neither of them was Maud, anyway.

Georg stood up as well. He adjusted his glasses and took the chance to brush an invisible hair from his eyebrow. The woman smelled faintly of some fresh, cool perfume, and she had a small brooch on the lapel of her jacket, a flower or wreath of some sort. I wondered if it meant anything, or was simply supposed to be attractive. She sat down on the chair next to Georg without leaning back in it, put a file on her lap and glanced at the papers Georg was leafing through. Now and then the corner of her mouth twitched in an extremely professional smile.

"Yes . . ." Georg said. "It's a good life."

"Yes, it is."

The pair of them looked up at me, rather surprised, as if they hadn't been expecting an answer. Georg quickly went back to looking through his papers, and the woman with the bank-name looked at hers.

"It's going to be an awful lot of money," he said.

"Yes, I suppose you . . ." I began again, before I realised that he was addressing her the whole time. This was a conversation between the two of them. Clearly they were going to discuss the material before I was given the opportunity to comment on anything.

The woman with the bank-name nodded and smiled again. Slightly indulgently this time. Then she turned back to Georg.

"Who compiled the summary?"

"Someone called Maud," Georg said.

"Maud?"

"Yes, it says Maud Andersson here, must be someone down on the second floor . . ."

The woman with the bank-name ran her pen along the lines of Maud's report and worked her way through column after column, reading quickly in a fairly low voice.

"Okay, a clean sweep of H. C.s, across the board, high E. H. points since the age of twelve, no empathy inhibitors. Parents both deceased, no family of his own, but regular experience quotient from comparable relationships. No setbacks noted since last December. Zero poverty rating. Top score on the emotional quotient . . . A number of good friendships over the years, all high engagement. Also an uncle — full marks as a role model. The child's response regarding the subject is fully emotional. Reliable, but with no great responsibilities . . . Strong emotional attachments without any pressure to achieve."

She moved on through the file, still pointing with her pen.

"Besides the welfare premium, whiteness premium, male premium, there's also . . . let's see . . . No problems sleeping. Workplace compatibility one hundred per cent. One old friend — Roger — who visits regularly, but no social obligations. In other words, nothing but positive attributes . . ."

I realised that none of this was really meant for my ears, but somehow it was rather wonderful to hear my life described that way. Almost impressive. I thought it sounded as if Maud had summarised my life in an extremely elegant way, and I couldn't help noticing that Georg raised his eyebrows a few times.

The woman with the bank-name sat there straight-backed throughout in a way that I thought must be uncomfortable, but presumably she was used to it because she didn't look at all troubled.

She had quite a small face, which made her eyes look disproportionately large behind a pair of glasses with heavy black frames. She might not have been conventionally beautiful, but there was something about her that commanded respect, which itself could probably be regarded as attractive, I reasoned. And if her lips had been filled, there was no denying that it was a very good job.

"Art? Culture?" Georg muttered.

"High musical receptiveness," she went on, reading out loud from Maud's report. "Responds positively. Affected by stimuli of the simplest harmonic variety."

"Payment capacity?" Georg said, and the woman leafed through her papers and pulled out another sheet.

"According to the report, extremely low, no private wealth, although no home inventory has been carried out . . . yet . . . even if the respondent declares that he has . . . let's see . . . 'instruments'."

She put a hand to her mouth as she cleared her throat. Or suppressed a giggle.

"And a small collection of science-fiction literature. Value unknown."

Georg turned to me at last.

"Well, then ... And you haven't made any payments?"

Out of the corner of my eye I could see the woman with the bank-name glancing at the report, evidently unable to resist shaking her head. That could have annoyed me, but I was still too astonished that Maud knew so much about me and had summarised it so nicely in that document.

"Er, no ..." I said.

He frowned and hummed to himself as he carried on looking through his papers.

"It's fairly unusual for people with similar scores to you not to have any money," he finally said. "Your category mostly consists of people with relatively large assets. Some, of course, were born with a silver spoon in their mouths, which is also one reason why their scores are so high — it all forms part of the same picture, so to speak. But even if they weren't born rich, their Experienced Happiness often gives them a certain excess of energy, if I can put it like that. This is usually reflected in financial gain. But with you ... the situation seems rather different ..."

"Yes," I said, and laughed, holding out my hands.

Georg fixed his eyes on me.

"You do understand how much money we're talking about here?" he said.

I slowly shook my head and blew some air out of my mouth.

"Not really . . ." I said, and laughed again.

Georg didn't look remotely amused. The woman with the bank-name pulled out one of the documents and inspected it more closely.

"You owe 5,700,150 kronor," Georg went on. "The interest alone will swallow up everything you could ever earn. Where do you work?"

I stretched and tried to adopt a confidence-inspiring expression, but the situation was somehow too absurd to really take in.

"At the moment I'm working part time at . . . Jugge's Flicks."

"*Jugge's?*" Georg said, and both I and the woman nodded. He looked at me sceptically, then turned towards her again.

"We'll have to arrange a home inventory as soon as possible," he said.

But she didn't respond. She was fully absorbed in something in the file. She leafed back and forth, comparing different sheets. She made a note of something. In the absence of any response he turned back to me. He put down his pen, sighed and rubbed his eyes.

"How on earth could you have failed to notice you had to pay?" he said. "You don't live in the middle of a forest, do you?"

"No," I chuckled.

"It can be extremely hard to reach people living in isolated shacks," he went on seriously. "People in the

60

desert or up in the mountains who don't have any direct contact with the outside world. Obviously that doesn't happen too often in our department, but you can imagine . . ."

I nodded.

"The information has to be gathered somehow."

"Of course," I said.

He ran a hand through his hair, squinted and looked at me carefully as if he thought I was some sort of interesting aberration.

"Do you have a television?" he asked.

I nodded.

"So how could you . . .?"

He held up a hand and counted on his fingers.

"Our information campaign, all the discussions . . . the whole debate."

"I really don't watch much television," I said.

"Really?" he said.

"I mean, it's not as if I've got anything against television," I said. "Quite the opposite."

I thought about how easily I got distracted by practically any programme. No matter what it was about. I got drawn in and fascinated by pretty much any moving pictures. The most obscure little broadcast, the most niche interest, could capture my attention and carry me off to other worlds — the more out of the ordinary, the more interesting I found it.

"Still, I think I ought to clarify . . ." I went on. "I mean, I really do think, if you make a proper comparison . . . I think I should point out . . ."

Even though I was trying, I couldn't really come up with a good way to finish the sentence.

"Hmm," Georg said wearily, looking at me. "You're questioning our calculations?"

"Well, I just think . . . er, I don't know."

He waited to see if I had anything else to add. When nothing appeared he leaned back in his chair, crossed one leg over the other and said in an authoritative voice, "Our calculations have been developed and refined over many, many years. This is an incredibly complex science, as I hope you can appreciate. This isn't just any old *felicific calculus*, you know."

He smiled faintly.

"Obviously it has its roots in Bentham's early theories, or, if you prefer, Pietro Verri . . ."

He laughed again. This was obviously highly amusing.

"But in recent years we have developed a much more finely calibrated set of tools. Of course, we have access to a vast amount of information. Obviously this is all more than a mere mortal can hope to gain an overview of, but the programme deals with the constituent parts in an extremely sensitive way, and, when taken in context, each aspect can be calculated with a good degree of accuracy. For instance, we use both cardinal and ordinal measures."

He brought his fingertips together.

"Instruments of this complexity give us the possibility to evaluate each individual's results. So when the main decision about international redistribution was taken . . ."

He held out one hand.

". . . well, we were all ready to get going."

I nodded as if I understood. As if I had even the slightest idea of who these men were and what their theories meant. Verri? Sounded like a footballer. Georg gathered his papers together and looked at the time.

"You'll have to stick around for the next few days and wait for the investigators," he said, and made to stand up.

"Hold on a moment," the woman with the bank-name said. She pushed one file towards Georg.

"Take a look at this," she went on, holding out another sheet of paper and placing it on top of the first. "It doesn't match."

She and Georg both inspected the figures one more time. Looking from file to file and comparing amounts. The tips of her fingers slid silently across the paper.

"Who did these calculations?" she asked.

"Well, it came from Twelve, so it must have been the economists in . . ."

Georg started to look for a signature on the sheet of calculations as the woman talked, half to herself, half to Georg.

"Look at this, here . . ."

She pointed at one column, then moved her hand to another sheet of paper.

"And then compare it with this . . ."

They both hunched over the documents. I felt like taking a look as well, but thought it probably best to stay where I was. I had a feeling I wouldn't understand much of those numbers and diagrams anyway.

63

Georg ran a hand through his thin, tinted hair. The woman suddenly got to her feet and hurried out to the reception desk. She came back with a calculator and apologised.

"I'm terribly sorry," she said, "but there seems to have been some mistake here."

"No problem," I said. "I'm not in any hurry."

Georg took the calculator and tapped in some numbers.

"This isn't right at all," he muttered. They stared at each other.

I felt some of the pressure in my chest ease and my shoulders slowly began to relax. On some level I had always suspected that things couldn't really be as bad as all that. The amount was obviously far too high for it to have anything to do with me. With a bit of luck everything was going to get sorted out now.

"See here," she whispered. "They've added those two numbers to that one. That's why . . ."

She looked up at me and smiled again. Her face looked tenser now, making her smile look stiffer, more like a grimace.

"We really are terribly sorry," she said.

She put the pen down and tapped at the calculator.

"There's been a mistake . . . a miscalculation. The amount you need to pay isn't 5,700,000 kronor. It's . . ."

They both stared at the calculator.

". . . 10,480,000 kronor."

CHAPTER
TWELVE

When I got back to the flat everything seemed to have taken on a different tone. The whole place had changed. Everything suddenly looked colourless. It was as if I could see how cheap and simple it was for the first time. Shabby. I saw the empty pizza boxes sticking out of a paper bag, waiting to be taken out to the bin. The dirty dishes in the sink, the sun-bleached curtains, the sagging sofa.

The worn old thresholds I walked over day after day. The dust on the floor, table and window sills. The old, washed-out clothes scattered all over the place. But also the things I liked best of all: my flat-screen computer, the shelves of films, the games, the rug with the Heinz logo. The Beatles mug. My Asimov collection. The M. C. Escher poster, of that waterfall that seems to be flowing upwards, and which I had been saying was my favourite picture for several years. Now it just looked banal. Clichéd and ordinary. The old mirrored picture with the Coca-Cola logo, which, admittedly, had felt old and ridiculous for years, but nonetheless held so many memories. Sketchpads and pens. Some paintbrushes. My guitars. The Indian statues Sunita had given me. The big bookcase full of vinyl records and magazines.

The CD collection. The boxes of neatly arranged cassette tapes. The things that had been my most cherished possessions. Now the whole lot felt dead. Lifeless. Why had I kept all this stuff?

A menu for the Thai restaurant was stuck to the fridge door, with one from the pizzeria on the freezer. There were circles round the Calzone Special and Pompeii. My favourites. The two I could never choose between, before I always ended up ordering the Calzone. The same calendar I always bought, the one I felt comfortable with, was hanging from the inside of the open kitchen cupboard, completely blank. I felt like bursting into tears.

CHAPTER
THIRTEEN

The next day it was my turn to be back in the shop. It was fairly quiet. The tape in the kitchen had come loose and the door of the cupboard under the sink was hanging half-open as usual. I fiddled with it for a while until I got it to stick again, even though I knew it wouldn't last long. I made some coffee in the scorched jug as the peculiar events of the past few days buzzed round my head. It was difficult to make any sense of things. The astronomical amount of money, the strange way they talked at W. R. D. I wasn't used to that sort of thing. I couldn't help thinking that I really didn't want anything to change at all. Then I found myself thinking about the internet and changed my mind. Obviously there were some changes that were good, and some bad. But I realised it was sometimes hard to tell the difference. Dynamite, for instance: was that good or bad? I stood by the shelf of documentaries and reflected upon good and bad changes through the ages. As I thought about which ones had to be counted as the biggest changes over the years, I realised that I had a tendency to rank more recent changes above older ones. For instance, industrialisation above the invention of the wheel, or the telegraph above the shift to fixed human settlements. I ranked my personal three favourite changes in the western world during the past three centuries, and suddenly I was standing there with the BBC's documentary about the Suffragettes' struggle for women's votes in my hand. Then I came across a film called *Iron Jawed Angels*. It looked good. I must remember to watch it. And Tom Baker would soon be releasing a new film called *The Voice*, which had to be about Frank Sinatra, I thought. Unless it was about Ella Fitzgerald? Perhaps it was about that talent show? Then I came up with a new way of puffing out my cheeks and amused myself with that for a while.

After that I found the remains of an old sticker that someone had stuck to the side of the counter, now just fragments that it was quite fun to pick off with my thumb and forefinger. Twenty minutes or so later, I'd almost managed to get rid of it all.

I called and ordered a Thai takeaway, and just after lunch a red-haired girl came in with a whole bundle of films she was returning late. She was in a bad mood, and thought we should have sent a reminder. I said we usually did just that, but she shook her head and said she hadn't received one.

"Well, that sort of thing happens sometimes," I said. "There might be something wrong with the computer . . ."

We agreed to drop the fine for late return, seeing as there had obviously been a problem with the reminder, and she looked a bit happier when she left.

I wondered if she'd received a huge bill from W. R. D. as well. I reasoned that we should probably try to keep each other's mood up as best we could. Set a good example to each other. Eventually things would slip back into some sort of everyday routine again. Somehow it felt slightly reassuring to know that we were all in the same boat. She was pretty when she smiled, I thought. Freckles can be very attractive.

A bit later that afternoon I stuck an old video into the little television with a built-in VHS player behind the counter, and had time to watch the first half of *Blade Runner* before finishing for the day. As I shut and locked the shop I remembered that I had been planning to change the background on my phone again, but hadn't got round to it. Oh well, I thought. That's something else I can still do.

On the way home I walked past one of those big advertising hoardings. "Give or take", it said in big blue letters. For the first time I noticed the name of the advertiser, their logo printed in the right-hand corner. Letters that were so wide and stylised that they didn't really look like text. Three cubes with just tiny differences to indicate the separate letters. The first was a very solid crown, and the other two like boxes with lines and dots on. Only if you looked closely and, like me, had spent a lot of time over the past few days in the company of that acronym, could you make out the letters W, R and D.

CHAPTER
FOURTEEN

I got home just before seven, and had started leafing through the latest catalogue from an IT company when my phone buzzed in my pocket. For some reason I thought it was Maud, but when I answered I heard Roger's breathless voice at the other end.

"Hi! Have you had yours?"

"What?" I said.

"Invoice. Have you had yours?"

It sounded almost like he was running. He probably wasn't, but his way of sighing as he spoke, combined with his general poor fitness, made it sound like he was.

"Hang on," he said, as if he'd just remembered something he had to do. "There's someone here . . . Can you call me back?" He hung up.

Roger had always been very careful with money. Presumably he was worried about being poor or feeling exploited, unless it was just in his genes. And apart from adopting various rituals to save money — the sort all really mean people do, like never leaving tips, taking his own bags to the shops, reusing unfranked stamps and old envelopes, turning the car engine off when he was going downhill, all the usual stuff — he had also got into the habit of never making phone calls and waiting for people to call him instead. No matter how urgent it was. If he ever did have to make a call, he made sure he started the conversation, then broke off quickly so the person he had called would have to phone him back.

He answered on the first ring.

"Yes," I said, lying down on the sofa.

"It's unbelievable, isn't it?" Roger panted. "What the hell's it all about? As if there wasn't enough shit to deal with already. Now they want even more money. It's insane. Don't you think? Completely insane."

I put both legs up on the armrest. It struck me that I almost always lay down when I talked to him. As if I had a particular posture for conversations with Roger.

"Yes, it is."

There was a crackling, knocking sound down the line, as if he'd dropped his phone or bumped into something. He never did just one thing at a time. He was always busy doing things that no one else really understood. He had the ability to sound in a hurry even though he didn't have a job, or anything else he had to do.

"Hello?" he said after a while.

"Yes," I said.

"I mean, it's completely unbelievable. Isn't it? You think this sort of thing only happens to people who are well off. Now I've got to get a bank loan and all that crap. I'm going to have to mortgage the boat or something . . . Are you still there?"

I said I was, as Roger battled on with whatever he was doing. It sounded like he was out in the wind. Were there people in the background? Maybe he'd gone down to the marina to look at his main asset. At first it felt rather reassuring that even Roger was going to have to make some sort of sacrifice. It felt good to have someone I could share my worries with. A man with his attitude to money must be completely beside himself at receiving an invoice like that. It must have hit him like a bomb.

Roger had a very nice sailing boat that he took good care of. It was his passion. He would take me out on it in the summer. In return for a contribution to the cost of the petrol for the engine and as long as I brought food, beer and so on. We usuatly ended up floating about in some inlet somewhere. Drinking beer and watching the birds. But even though it was nice, it was still a fairly small boat. Six or seven metres at most. How much would he be able to borrow against that?

I put my legs back down and sat up.

"How much was yours, then?" I asked.

"What?" he panted as he fiddled with something. His voice sounded muffled and distant. I could tell he'd wedged his phone between his ear and his shoulder.

"How much have you got to pay?" I said.

"A fuck of a lot," he said in a loud voice, to make himself heard over the sound of an engine in the background.

I stood up.

"How much?"

"220,000 kronor."

CHAPTER
FIFTEEN

The sun was going down over the city, casting dazzling reflections off the rooftops. It was still so warm that I had the windows wide open. I could hear the rowdy voices of children playing football or hockey down in the street. Their warning cries to each other whenever a car appeared. How could I possibly have ended up being charged so much more than Roger? There had to have been some sort of mistake. They must have missed something. Maybe they'd got me confused with some rich kid from the Wallenberg set? Or some oligarch. Admittedly, Roger was a tragic loser with no income and no prospects. Obviously I would have expected to have to pay more than him, anything else would have been very odd. But this? This was unbelievable.

I did a quick run-through of the problems and setbacks I'd experienced in my life, and decided that I was far too wretched to warrant this new amount of 10,480,000 kronor.

I lay down on the sofa and thought about how much I missed my parents. This was precisely the sort of time I'd have called them to say I was in trouble. I'd have a bit of a moan, and they would have listened carefully with the phone between them, then they'd have comforted me and said that everything would be all right. And then it would have been. I felt an intense longing for the warm, fluffy feeling that always blossomed in me as soon as I'd dumped a problem on them. Then I could have curled up in my pyjamas in front of the television with a bag of cheesy puffs. I thought about all my friends. They'd long since got married and had kids, and they barely had time to see me any more. What had once been deep friendships and endless days of unconditional socialising and spontaneous outings, weeks of shared discoveries — at one time they were the only fixed point in my life — long conversations, discussions about politics and relationships and the world . . . All of that had soon been reduced to a snatched cup of coffee in passing or a quick beer once every six months. The only one left was Roger, who had never seemed to be able to make much sense of life. He never really offered any resistance to anything, and was no great support. As time passed he was getting increasingly stressed about growing older, and the fact that he never had time for anything, that nothing ever really happened. But at the same time he never seemed able to work out how he wanted things, and just sank deeper and deeper into self-loathing and an increasingly unhealthy attitude towards money.

He always managed to feel hard done by. It was as if he assumed he was going to end up the loser, even if things actually looked okay. With the passage of time he would turn his successes into failures, like some

74

back-to-front version of Buddhism. Any unexpected moments of happiness always carried with them a measure of unease, which eventually took over. Once, a long time ago, his beloved boat fell off its winter stand on the quayside, and ended up with a big hole in one side of the hull. "It's a fucking nightmare," Roger said. "It's going to cost tens of thousands to repair." After some investigation, it turned out that the crane-driver had knocked into the stand earlier that winter, and that the marina was therefore obliged to pay for the damage. A conflict flared up between the marina, the crane-driver and the insurance company. Each thought that one of the others was liable.

"Typical," Roger said when he finally got me to call him. "Now no one wants to pay. It's going to cost me tens of thousands of kronor."

He spent all winter going on about how many tens of thousands of kronor it was going to cost him. Eventually the insurance company agreed that it was their responsibility and that Roger would get full compensation for the damage. When the hull was being repaired, it turned out that it made more sense to replace a good part of the deck as well. A highly professional boat company did the work very thoroughly, and in plenty of time before the sailing season began. To smooth things over, the marina offered to waive the rent for the following year. So when it came down to it, Roger had actually gained from the whole business. But he still went on referring to it as a huge disaster, and took it as proof that only bad things ever happened to him. "Do you know," he would often say, even years later, "the whole thing cost tens of thousands of kronor."

For the first time in a long time I missed having a girlfriend. I found myself thinking about Sunita, and felt a tug at my heart. I thought about the evenings we spent in her beautiful flat in Vasastan. It was really her father's, but because he worked in Mexico and the rest of the family lived in India it was basically hers. When we were together it had almost felt like mine. Even though I always knew that our relationship was finite.

We met at the film club at the university, where she was studying. The members were mostly foreign students, and the club organised a programme of screenings of Swedish classics on Monday evenings. Bergman, Sjöberg, and so on. I was invited to come and run the sessions. The film club offered wine, and I would give a short talk about that week's director, explaining recurrent themes, showing stills and short clips, and on the whole I enjoyed doing it. Each Monday evening after the movie, Sunita and I would stand there looking at one another, and in the end I asked her where she was from, and she told me, not without a degree of pride and in surprisingly broken English, that she was from the holy city of Varanasi, but had grown up in Bombay. That pride, combined with a very fetching degree of shyness, made an indelible impression on me. She seemed so incredibly exotic. Maybe I seemed the same to her. We never spoke anything but English, but I think she knew a bit of Swedish, even if she pretended she didn't. She loved films, and Bergman in particular. I managed to get hold of special editions with extra material, and we spent hour after hour in front of the television in her big living room, on an enormous soft white sofa.

Sunita's father was a diplomat. He had recently been transferred from Sweden to Mexico, but for some reason he didn't want Sunita to go with him. Maybe he thought she should finish her education first. It was probably also to do with the fact that she had an uncle who lived in Sweden who could act as a combination of guardian and chaperone, albeit from a distance. And presumably they also reasoned that it was safer for Sunita here. They hadn't counted on me.

Sunita was the apple of her father's eye, and the affection was mutual. Time and time again I heard about how great this father of hers was. That all Indians only wanted sons, but that her mother and father had been happy when they had a daughter. That it was extremely unusual for a daughter to be allowed to travel and study. Sunita always said she loved her father above everything and everyone else, and because he was such a distant presence I had no problem with that.

Her relationship with me had to be kept secret, under all circumstances. No one must know anything. Not our families, and not our friends. I wasn't allowed to breathe a word about our relationship to my friends or anyone else I knew. She had been granted a few years to study and see the world, but she would have to go home and get married before she turned twenty-five. That was non-negotiable. The family already had a number of candidates lined up back at home. I never really understood the point of that whole tradition of arranged marriage and the caste-system, apart from the fact that it was the father who took the decisions, and that she belonged to a higher caste than most people and that this fling with me would be regarded as absolutely inconceivable. The sort of thing that simply didn't happen. It was so far beyond the bounds of possibility that it was unthinkable.

Eventually the whole family would be reunited back in India. But in the meantime she was able to live a relatively free life here in Sweden. The only requirement was that she studied hard and was still a virgin when she returned to Bombay.

She wasn't.

She was very careful to start with. Me too. We talked a lot. Mostly about films, but gradually more and more about each other. She would light candles and incense. She had dark eyes — almond-shaped, that's what people say, isn't it? — and incredibly soft skin. Long hair, and oddly full cheeks given the fact that she was otherwise fairly slender. She often complained that her backside was too broad, and that her nose was too big, but she was actually astonishingly beautiful. I loved just looking at her. I told her, and I think she rather liked the fact that I did that. She was always beautifully dressed, in green, yellow and red fabrics that looked extremely expensive.

We took every precaution we could. We never spoke to each other in public, and rarely let anyone see us together. We never phoned each other, and came up with a special code and secret signs that no one else would be able to understand. A twist of a bracelet would mean that there was a sealed letter at the reception desk where I came and went fairly regularly to pick up films and packages for the film club. To start with they were just short messages: "9 p.m.", for instance. Which meant that at nine o'clock precisely I would step through the door on the other side of her block, cross the courtyard and be let into her apartment a couple of minutes later. Never any knocking on doors. Never any doorbell.

Once we were there we would stand for a while in the big living room, just looking at the view. We would talk about the weather and university, maybe about something that had happened. Sometimes she would offer me mineral water or juice of some sort. Then she would very slowly start to take off her thin layers of clothing, almost in passing, while we talked about something else or watched a film. When the film was over we would sit still and just wait. Breathing. Inhaling each other's scent. Looking into each other's eyes. Sometimes for several minutes. I never imagined I would ever meet a woman like her. In a way, I was just happy to be near her, but the prohibition of love and our mutual caution — the tentative way we approached each other physically — meant that the air in the room was charged with desire.

Only after a number of weeks did we actually touch one another, slow, feather-light strokes, and it was even longer before we kissed. Slowly but surely we shifted the boundary of what was permissible. Once or twice relatives or guardians or governesses or whatever they were showed up. On one occasion, the state I was in meant that I had to hide on the balcony. Otherwise, I was a special tutor who was helping her with her studies. Maybe I was given a title and name, I don't know. They would spend a long time talking. I didn't understand a word, but to judge from their behaviour it looked like they accepted her explanation. That uncle of hers never appeared. Maybe he had people who checked up on her for him. Either way, everyone seemed happy, and she remained unsullied in their eyes. None of them seemed able even to entertain the thought that anything untoward might be taking place in that apartment. Which was ridiculous — we were young, after all.

As time passed our messages became more and more refined. Sometimes the letters contained gifts. Serviettes or a box of matches bearing the address of a certain restaurant. That didn't mean that she and I were going to meet there, but that I was welcome to look in and pick up a signal about what might happen later that evening.

Sometimes I would find the place and sit down alone at a suitable distance, and watch her dine with one or more of her relatives or whoever they were. If she twisted her bracelet a specific number of times, that was a sign that it was okay to go back to hers afterwards, as long as I waited until the coast was clear before creeping in the back way and being let in for a late-night rendezvous.

As we grew more comfortable with the arrangement, she also became more provocative. Once there was a padded envelope waiting at the reception desk. Inside was a note with a time and the address of a smart restaurant, plus an item of clothing which she wanted me to understand that she wouldn't be wearing beneath her brightly coloured sarong that evening as she ate dinner with three elderly ladies and a gentleman who all looked like they were liable to fall asleep at any moment. I sat five tables away and couldn't bring myself to order anything but a Coke, which was a blessing seeing as even that turned out to cost three times as much as I thought it was possible for a soft drink to cost. At one point during the evening she glanced in my direction and looked me in the eye for a long moment. Suddenly I began to worry that she had twisted her bracelet and that I had missed it. I was sure I had noticed some sort of movement, but perhaps she had just been checking the time? I sat there for a long while with ice cubes in my mouth, just staring at her in the hope of picking up a more obvious signal. But none came. Just to be sure, I went to her apartment anyway. I stood there on the landing, thinking I could hear her inside, but the door never opened.

She had an ability to smile with her whole face when she looked at me, as if she could see past the mask, past my ordinary, everyday self. Sometimes when we were lying in bed she would trace the features of my face with her finger. From my hairline, down across my

81

forehead and nose, over my chin and down to my chest. It was like a film.

I was never allowed to sleep there. When it was late enough, I had to gather my clothes together and get dressed, then creep out the same way I had come in.

When Sunita had turned twenty-four and finished her degree, the anticipated command arrived from Mexico telling her to move back to Bombay to get married, and Sunita didn't hesitate for a second. She was conditioned to obey her family's wishes, and constantly surprised me with her loyalty to a system which — in my world, at least — could only be regarded as oppressive. She was utterly faithful to her father's wishes, and just got angry if I questioned any part of the arrangements. She was proud of her roots and who she was, and it would never occur to her to want to change anything. And that was something that no arguments about gender equality or fleeting erotic adventures would change.

On our last night together, we made love and cried the whole time, and the next day we stood at Arlanda Airport separated by a safe distance of thirty metres. Between us we had all her many relatives and hundreds of passing strangers.

A brief glance, then she was gone.

It took me several years before I could really think about anything else. I imbued all music with my own heartfelt sorrow, compared every sad lyric with my memories of us. Every so often I would wake in the middle of the night and imagine that she was there beside me. But each time the bed was empty. Sometimes I would walk past one of the restaurants she had sat in and imagine that I could see her, but it was always someone else.

I slowly sat up on the sofa. I ran my hands through my hair and wondered if I had ever really got over her. Since Sunita I hadn't had any long relationships. I compared all women to her. I searched in vain for that spark, that intensity . . .

I realised I was never going to experience that sort of erotic charge and intense tenderness again. Occasionally I wondered if she still thought about me. Did she remember me? Did she remember any of our adventures and secret meetings, or had she suppressed it all? On some level she must still miss what we had. A bit, at any rate. How much had she and her family had to pay to W. R. D.?

The sun had gone down. It was dark inside the flat, but I couldn't be bothered to switch on any lamps. I alternated between lying down and glaring at my worthless possessions, and sitting up and scratching my head. Evening passed and turned into night. I ought to have gone to bed, but I could just feel myself getting more and more upset.

CHAPTER
SIXTEEN

"I don't understand," I said to Maud when she eventually picked up, sounding slightly drowsy. "I don't think this is fair at all."

I heard her clear her throat at the other end of the line.

"No . . . hmm . . . I heard that your amount had been adjusted," she said.

It was the middle of the night. Maybe she was trying to get some rest between calls. Maybe she'd actually dozed off? Obviously even she needed to sleep sometimes. Either way, right then I didn't care. I'd been lying on the sofa for hours, getting worked up about the unfair calculation. I felt I had to vent my frustration.

"Adjusted?" I said. "It was doubled!"

She was moving something. A duvet, maybe, or a blanket.

"Yes, I looked through your file afterwards and, well, it's an impressive result, I have to admit. They managed to get your figures badly wrong upstairs in —"

"But my friend Roger —" I interrupted her, before she immediately interrupted me, as usual with a practised harangue. She could probably do it in her sleep.

"It's best not to try to make comparisons," she said. "It's incredibly hard to see the differences if you haven't been trained and understand the system."

I didn't care about that now. I felt like I'd heard enough.

"I think it's deeply unfair," I went on. "The more I think about it, the worse I feel. I mean, I haven't done anything at all with my life. Not a thing. I haven't travelled or studied or applied myself to anything . . . I used to drift about with my mates and talk a lot of rubbish and hang out at bars. And now I sit here every day watching films or playing games or listening to music. In the past few years I've always gone to the same supermarket and bought the same cereal for breakfast. I get the same coffee from the same café, I still work at the same place, and I basically stand there doing the same thing every day. Then I go to the same restaurant and get a takeaway. I even go to the same kiosk when I want ice-cream. I usually grab a Pizza Grandiosa, 'X-tra everything, 40% more taste', and heat it up in the microwave. If I want to push the boat out I buy a Nogger ice-lolly for dessert. Two, even. I never go out. I don't see any friends. That's no sort of life!"

"Why don't you go out?" Maud said.

She sounded more alert, but her voice was still a bit hoarse. More than usual, anyway. For a moment I caught myself wondering if she was wearing night clothes. How did she prefer to sleep? At the same time, I was too upset really to think about her like that. For once, I was just too angry. Sad, even. And I noted how effectively that strangled any tendency towards flirtation.

"I don't know," I said. "I hadn't thought about it until after I spoke to you. You tell me I have to pay because I've had it so easy, but in actual fact I've had a really shit time."

"But you had all the prerequisites for . . ." she began.

"That just makes it worse," I said.

I could feel I wasn't far from bursting into tears, at the thought of all the things I could have done. Sunita — should I have chased after her? Should I have gone to India and found out where she lived and tried to take her away from there with me? Where to? Back to Sweden? To live in my flat, as the partner of a part-time shop assistant at Jugge's Flicks? Would she have agreed to that? Tears pricked my eyes, making me sound more strident. It probably came out more aggressively than I intended.

"That's the saddest thing of all. I had every opportunity, but what the hell have I done? Nothing. Nada. Not a damn thing."

Maybe she was scared, or just worried that I was going to start crying over the phone, but she sounded much softer now.

"How did that happen, then?"

"How the hell should I know?" I said. "It just did. The years passed. You don't think. Everything's all nice and familiar, and I suppose I'm frightened of getting hurt or something . . . I don't know . . . I've always avoided conflict, and I've always been really happy if I could get away without quarrelling with people. Before,

86

I used to be happy when I managed to avoid things, it felt like some sort of victory, you know, like I'd got away with something and didn't have to do something I didn't want to. Like being let off homework at school, or managing not to get beaten up in the playground. But now . . . God, I don't know, it feels like I've been fooled somehow, as if everything I avoided was actually . . ."

I could feel my eyes stinging.

"Well . . . actually life itself."

I couldn't hold back any more. I started to howl down the phone. Bellowing like an animal. I didn't care what she thought. She was welcome to think it was unattractive and awkward. Oddly enough, she didn't seem remotely worried. Quite the contrary. She said in a gentle voice: "So what would you like to do?"

I lay down on the floor on my back. Looked up at the ceiling and tried to breathe calmly. The floorboards actually felt fairly cool.

"I don't know," I said. "Anything. I might have liked to travel, meet people. More girls. Tried different things . . . You know, maybe do something illegal . . ."

I closed my eyes and snorted the snot back into my nose.

"Nothing, really. I suppose I should just have been more aware of what I did have. I mean, we talked about the sun and all that before . . ."

"You said you liked the view," she said.

I noticed that I had raised my voice.

"Exactly. So why the hell didn't I go outside? Why didn't I take the chance to enjoy everything a bit more?"

"Why didn't you?"

I stared up at the ceiling. There were cracks in it. Hard to see where they started. It was like it had cracked in several different places at the same time. I found myself thinking about really old porcelain. After a while I lowered my head to stretch my neck.

"I don't know," I said. "I suppose I'm just a — what do they call it? — a creature of habit."

"Yes, we've noticed."

"What? How?"

"I mean, our inspectors."

I stretched my neck some more, back and forth, grateful for the hard floor that didn't move when I did. It was nice. Almost like a massage.

"Inspectors?" I said.

"They're the ones who give us information. They've also noticed that you're — how shall I put it? — a person of regular habits."

"Horribly regular," I said with a snort. "It hasn't struck me before, but it's pretty damn tragic."

I rested my head back on the floor.

"Are you being honest now?" Maud asked.

"Yes," I said, clearing my throat to get my voice back under control.

"I mean, this isn't just something you're saying to get the debt down? Like when you said you were anxious?"

"No."

I lay there on the floor thinking. Thinking about life. About all the times, the moments, that were gone for good. All the encounters and people. Quite without warning I realised that tears were welling up in my eyes again without me being able to do anything to stop them.

"And I miss my mum," I said in a cracked voice. She said nothing for a while. Just waited. Let me catch my breath.

"You were very fond of your mother," she said, more as a statement than a question. I couldn't bring myself to answer. I nodded to myself and sniffed.

We were both silent for a few minutes. I couldn't remember the last time I'd opened up to anyone like this. It felt good, in a way. Like a new me. She didn't seem to have anything against it. She could have hung up if she didn't want to listen. But she let me go on.

"We went camping one summer in Närke," I said.

"I know," she said. "I saw."

"You did?" I said. "Yes, of course you did."

"Let's see, 1984, wasn't it?" she said, but corrected herself immediately. "No, '85."

"Probably," I said, trying to wipe the tears from my cheeks. "It rained the whole time," I added, for safety's sake.

"Yes, I saw that as well," Maud mumbled.

"Mum and me. And Dad and my sister, of course . . . We hired a caravan."

"A mobile home, wasn't it?" Maud said. "The year before you hired a caravan. A Cabby, Model 532. In 1985 you had . . . Ah. Sorry. You were about to say something . . ."

I went and got a piece of kitchen roll to blow my nose on.

"Right, yes, a mobile home."

We said nothing for a bit. I blew my nose as quietly as I could.

"Did you like the rain?" she said.

"Well, I don't like it when it rains non-stop . . ."

"No, of course not, but on that occasion it seemed to match your profile."

"Really? Yes, it was nice sitting there. We didn't really do much. We just . . . Well, what can I say? We just *were*."

I heard her leaf through her file again.

"Hmm. Yes, you score very highly for that week. Health, relationships, intensity, the oxygen content of the air . . . Yes, across the board, actually."

"We played Uno," I said, feeling that I was about to burst into tears again.

"Sorry?"

"Uno," I said. "That's what we played."

She said nothing for a moment.

"Oh. What's that?"

"Uno. It's a game. You've never heard of it?"

"No, I haven't, actually. Is it like Monopoly?"

"Sort of, but easier."

"What's the point of it?"

I couldn't help smiling.

"What's the *point* of it?"

She sounded suddenly bewildered.

"Yes?" she said bluntly.

"I can't actually remember any more. I think you have to get rid of your cards or something. Well, it's not important. You've never played Uno, then?"

"No."

"We should try it one day," I said.

She didn't answer.

CHAPTER
SEVENTEEN

It was somehow easier to talk to her now. It felt more like talking to a friend. Even if she was still using that factual tone of voice. I realised that to her ears I must sound like an extremely sensitive, intuitive person. She was so correct. So definite. I suddenly got the impression that I was the opposite. But what did that mean? Wrong? And abstract?

"You're good at Sporcle," she said. "You get very high scores. Especially on film titles and directors."

"Too right!" I said. "I'm right up there . . . well . . . somewhere in the middle."

She laughed.

"You don't have to cover up anything," she said. "Anyway, we've already got the information."

"Mmm," I said. "Okay, I'm pretty good."

I ran my hand across the floor. I ended up with a pale grey strand of dust on my fingertips. I really should get the hoover out.

"Is it fun, your job?" I asked after a pause.

"I'm not sure about fun," she said. "It's exciting to be part of the big change, and the work feels useful . . . I mean, it's an important task . . ."

"That Georg," I said.

"Yes?"

"He's . . . What's he like?"

She thought for a moment.

"I don't know the people up there very well. But as far as I know, he's smart, and knows the procedures very well. Out of everyone at W. R. D., he's probably the one who's best at —"

"Does he dye his hair?"

She fell silent again.

"Hmm . . ." she began. "Does he dye his hair? I don't actually know."

"I bet he does," I said. "He reminds me of a character in a film."

"Oh?" she said.

"I just can't remember which one."

I crumpled the piece of kitchen roll into a ball and dabbed my cheeks again.

"Have you always liked films?" she asked after a brief pause.

I sniffed a yes down the phone.

"How long have you worked in the video shop?"

I thought she ought to have that in her flies, but took a deep breath and thought about it. I cleared my throat and made an attempt to steady my voice.

"Er," I said, "it must be nine years now."

She said nothing at first, as if she too was wondering if this really sounded like a ten-million-kronor life.

"So what's your favourite film?" she asked eventually.

"My favourite film? Oh, I don't know, it's so hard to choose. I almost always think there's something good in every film . . ."

I could hear her smiling at the other end.

"I could have guessed that," she said.

"I mean, it's so hard to pick just *one* film."

She muttered in what could been agreement, or just an indication that she knew I was going to say that as well.

"But there is one scene," I said, after a pause. "In a Bosnian film called *The Bridge*."

"*The Bridge?*"

"Yes, it isn't a very well-known film. You probably haven't seen it, but . . . it's, I don't know . . . I often think about that scene."

"Why do you do that?"

"It's . . . How can I put it? It's good. It's a good scene. Anyway, what's your favourite film?"

She coughed.

"Mine?" she said. "Oh, I don't watch a lot of films."

I was on the point of saying I could have guessed that, but stopped myself.

"But you must have seen some?"

"Well," she said, "nothing very memorable."

"So what do you do, then?"

"Me?"

"Yes."

"I work," she said quickly, and laughed.

I joined in. These conversations of ours were starting to feel fairy intimate. As if we'd crossed a boundary. As if we could talk about things that really mattered. Openly and honestly. Without embarrassment.

"No, but seriously?" I said.

She didn't reply at first.

"Well, I do work a lot, you know."

We both fell silent.

"So, what do you like most?" I eventually asked. "Films? Music?"

She laughed again. Unless it was more of a giggle.

"Art? Theatre, maybe?" I went on.

"No, not theatre," she said.

"No?"

"No, I don't know . . ."

"Books?"

More silence. It was obvious that she wasn't used to this sort of role reversal. She wasn't at all comfortable answering questions, and would much rather do the asking herself.

"What do you do to relax?" I persisted.

"Well," she said, "I like reading the paper . . ."

Another silence, and I didn't really know what to say. I let my eyes drift from the ceiling to the sofa with its threadbare cover. She made a rustling sound, then drank some more tea or coffee. I tried to imagine her at home. The silence was still fairly comfortable.

"What amount did you get?" I said.

"No," she said firmly. "We don't discuss our personal amounts with . . ."

She didn't finish the sentence, and I never found out what she was going to call someone like me.

"Okay," I said, "but you could still tell me, couldn't you?"

"It's completely against the rules for an employee to divulge . . ."

"How about bending the rules a bit?"

She didn't answer at first.

"Like I said, it's best not to make comparisons," she said. "It's not helpful."

"Maybe," I said. "But . . .?"

She was breathing through her nose. I imagined I could see her smiling.

"Well, it came to a fair bit," she said.

"How much?"

She laughed.

"Look, I really shouldn't . . ."

I could almost see her top lip curl. She was probably hoping I would leave it at that, that I would realise I had gone too far and drop the subject, but when I didn't say anything she finally came clean:

"700,000, more or less."

We were both silent for a while as the amount hovered in the air between us.

"But," I eventually said, "that's nothing!"

"Like I said, it's extremely difficult to make direct comparisons . . ."

I sat up.

"So what is it about you that means —"

She raised her voice as she interrupted me.

"Sorry, it was stupid of me to agree to this. I really don't want us to discuss my private —"

"But that's incredible," I went on. "What have I got that you —"

"Like I said, it's hard to see how everything fits together . . ."

"Why didn't you end up with a higher —"

She interrupted me again, loudly.

"I got a low score in affirmation! Okay?"

"Okay."

"My muscarinic cholinergic system doesn't allow for high results in certain areas," she said, then fell silent as if she thought I should make do with that as an explanation.

"Mmm," I said. "And in the sort of language you can actually understand?"

"I scored very low in the individual aspect. Low durability in the reward section."

I pondered those words for a moment.

"What does that mean?"

"That I'm bad at . . . Oh, I don't know . . ."

Then it was like she suddenly lost patience.

"What do you want me to say?! How am I supposed to explain this to you? There aren't any easier words! I'm just bad at . . ."

"Rewarding yourself?" I said.

She said nothing for a long time.

"You need to learn to *Experience*," I said.

She laughed.

"Like you?" she said.

"Like me," I said.

"Hmm. And look where that's got you . . ."

CHAPTER
EIGHTEEN

The windows were open while we talked. The night outside was still and warm. Nothing but the sound of a party in the distance. Funny how you can always recognise the sound, no matter how distant it is. Young people, perhaps thinking of going off for a swim in the moonlight, maybe staying up all night. Getting hold of some wine or beer and falling asleep together in a park somewhere as the first light of morning started to appear.

I asked if she sang, and at first she sounded irritated, as if she thought I was making fun of her. But when I said she had a good voice for jazz, and that it would be exciting to hear her sing, she laughed and said she'd think about it, that she didn't know much about jazz, and that there was absolutely no way it was going to happen that night. I don't know how long we talked to each other, but my cheek was starting to feel very hot, and I had to switch the phone to my other ear. It felt odd hearing her voice on that side.

"I think you should go to bed now," I said.

She laughed.

"Well, I tried that, but someone called and woke me up."

"So why do you always answer?"

She didn't say anything to that.

"You don't have to pick up," I said.

She still said nothing. But I could hear her breathing softly. Perhaps she was lying down. It felt like she was. I imagined I could see her in front of me, lying on her side, more or less the same as me, with the phone pressed against her cheek, her eyes closed.

"You've handled this really well," I said. "The other day I thought you'd written a really nice report about me. I'm very happy with the way you've dealt with me. I feel both informed and well looked after."

I heard her take a deep breath.

"Yes," she whispered. "But you're happy with so little . . ."

I pressed the phone closer to my ear.

"I think you deserve to switch that phone off now," I said.

Silence.

"If you don't want to talk, I mean . . ."

Another long silence. I put the phone in my other hand and carefully brushed some hair from my hot forehead.

"But if you do want to talk to me," I said, "we can do that. I think that would be lovely. I really like talking to you. But if you'd rather not, that's fine too. But I think my case has been dealt with now, to put it in professional terms or whatever it is. You just have to hang up and go to bed. I wouldn't think any the worse of you if you did."

She didn't make a sound. But she didn't hang up.

I lay down on the sofa and put the phone to my normal ear again.

"In *The Bridge*," I began, "close to the end of the film, it's so moving. They see each other in a café. Well . . ."

I wasn't sure if I should describe the scene, but something in the atmosphere, now that we were just sitting and listening to each other's silence, led me to carry on.

"They were lovers before . . . but they haven't seen each other for several years, for the entire duration of the war. Then suddenly, one day . . . She's there in the café and he just happens to pass by. There's something going on, I think they're both due in court . . . They can't let on that they know each other. The atmosphere is strained. Neither of them dares to speak. They're about to go to court. They're on different sides of the case. She's there with her family, who are the accused . . . He's there to give evidence against her brother or uncle or something. He catches sight of her from the square outside. And, as I said, they haven't seen each other for . . . actually, I'm not really sure. I don't remember the rest of the film that well. But it's been a while, anyway. Quite a long time. Several years. And suddenly there they are. He's standing. She's sitting down. Yes, that's it. She's sitting at a table in the café. And suddenly they catch sight of each other. They look at each other. Neither of them says anything. Neither of them does much at all, in fact. There's no big reaction, but rather the reverse: almost no reaction at all. But it still means so much. It's like a perfect example of a really good film-scene. If you watched it out of context you wouldn't understand a thing. You'd just see two people staring at each other. Not even that, in fact. Because they really don't do much. They look at each other and realise who the other is. I think he looks at his watch at one point. He realises that there's still plenty of time before the trial starts. He decides to sit down on the spare chair at the same table. And, well, a worse actress could have made a right mess of it by overacting and trying to show her old infatuation, anxiety, anguish or excitement, sadness, anything at all. But she doesn't. She doesn't move a muscle. Yet we still know exactly what she's feeling. And that's precisely why we know. They sit there for a long time, on either side of the table, next to each other, but both facing away. Watching people go past in the street. She raises her cup of tea or coffee or whatever it is at regular intervals. His arm is resting on the top of the table. He's holding a packet of cigarettes, and turns it every so often, standing it on end, then laying it down again. At one point a waiter comes over and takes on order, and then an old man comes over and talks to her. Presumably a relative. We don't hear what they say because there's music throughout the scene, but he's probably telling her it's time to head off to the courthouse. Once again, a less talented actor could have spoiled things by acting out too much anxiety or angst or whatever. But the man just sits there.

"Once the other man has left they just go on sitting like that, facing away from each other. Him with his arm on the table, holding the packet of cigarettes in his

101

hand. She's still holding her coffee cup. Suddenly he lets go of the cigarette packet and moves his hand a couple of centimetres towards her. Neither of them says anything. They both seem fully absorbed in watching the street. Gradually she moves her hand towards him, and for a moment the backs of their hands touch. One of her fingers trembles slightly. He takes a breath. Her little finger nudges his. That's all. It's so well done. It's so sensual. I mean, bloody hell, I can feel myself shiver just describing it."

Maud let out a laugh at the other end of the line.

"It sounds very good," she said.

"I know, it really is!" I said. "It's bloody brilliant!"

She laughed again.

We carried on talking until early in the morning. The sun rose slowly above the rooftops and shone its rays into the flat. Birds twittered as Maud talked more about her work. She revealed that she was hoping to get a position on the distribution committee, in phase two, when all the money was going to be shared out. I understood that she had been aiming for that the whole time, that that was what motivated her. I ended up listening to long descriptions of how the redistribution process would work, and tried to ask interesting follow-up questions.

We played a quiz on the subject of "me". Maud was unbelievably good at it, even if I suspected that she was cheating and looking at her files occasionally, although she claimed she was lying in bed and didn't have any professional material to hand.

"It's been a while," she laughed. "But I really am in bed now."

"Good!" I said.

We talked a bit about Roger, and Maud wondered if he was really a particularly good friend, and I had to explain that he did have his good sides, even if it was hard to spot them at first glance.

At some point in the early hours of the morning I asked if I could have her mobile number, so my calls wouldn't have to be redirected to her, but she said that was against the rules, they weren't allowed to give out any private numbers.

"They're very strict about that," she said.

Eventually the early birds began to emerge from their doorways down in the street. I could hear their rapid footsteps. The street-cleaners drove around, and slowly it got warmer and warmer inside the flat as we carried on chatting about all manner of things. We debated, laughed, disagreed with each other, fell silent, listening and waiting for the other to speak, the way I thought only teenagers did, and I could feel my head getting more and more fuzzy. The conversation became increasingly fragmented. I lurched from one emotion to the other. Laughed and cried. Lay there quietly and listened. Argued calmly at times, and held long, vaguely philosophical monologues. Every now and then I would lose my train of thought and stop abruptly in the middle of a sentence. Maud just seemed to get more and more giggly. It was nice to hear her like that. I began to worry about how she was going be able to cope with a day's work when she hadn't had any sleep, but decided not to broach the subject in case it led to her hanging up, because I didn't want that. Not now, when we seemed to have crossed some sort of line and anything seemed possible. Besides, she was a grown woman. Anyway, what did I know? Maybe she was on some sort of flexitime. She certainly gave the impression that she was perfectly capable of looking after herself. Considerably better than me, for instance.

I might have dozed off on the floor for a nanosecond. Perhaps Maud did as well. I felt tired, but in a good way. Drowsy, almost like being drunk. Every so often I would make an effort to pull myself together, and when Maud finally began to hint that it might be time to end the call, I got it into my head to try to summarise what I had meant to say at the outset.

"Okay, well, er . . ." I began, letting out a big yawn. "So, what now, then . . .? Do you think it would be feasible to . . .? I mean, it ought to be possible to correct my, er, E. H. score?"

I barely managed to get the sentence out, and Maud just giggled at me.

"Hmm . . . you mean change it?"

"Yes?"

"Based on what you've told me tonight?"

"Yes?"

"Hmm . . . No, I'm sorry."

We sat in silence for a while, and eventually I couldn't help laughing too. It was all just too much. I rolled onto my side and ended up with the phone pressed between my cheek and the floor.

"Oh, what the hell!" I said, and sighed. "I don't know. I suppose my life isn't that bloody awful."

"No?"

Now she sounded both amused and surprised.

"Well," I said, "I mean, it depends entirely on what expectations you have, doesn't it?"

"I think it sounds pretty good," she said.

I sighed again.

"Yes, but ten million kronor? Come on, I'd have thought you'd get a bit more for that sort of money . . ."

I got up on my knees, looked out through the window and caught sight of the pot plant on my neighbour's balcony. It was barely recognisable. The leaves were drooping over the edge of the pot, and there was something brown sticking up from the middle. I went and got a glass of water from the kitchen and tried to reach it with a few quick throws. Most of the water missed, and I wasn't sure if I was doing any good at all or just making the situation worse for the poor plant. I lay back down on the floor, took several deep breaths and suddenly felt a fresh wave of tears rising up inside me.

"And I can't help thinking about Sunita," I said. "It seems so incredibly tragic."

"Sunita?" Maud said.

"Yes, it was all a long while ago now, but I still find myself thinking about it the whole time. It still hurts . . ."

Instinctively I put my hand to my heart. As if she could see me. As if it could somehow emphasise the pain I felt.

"Sunita?"

"Yes."

"Who's Sunita?" Maud said in an entirely different tone of voice.

"Sunita. She was the great love of my life. We could have —"

Maud interrupted me.

"Hang on. We don't have any information about . . ."

"What?" I said.

I rolled onto my stomach and leaned my elbows on the floor. Down the line I could hear her get out of bed and tap at her computer.

"I haven't got anything about a Sunita," she said.

I got up on my knees, rubbed my eyes and tried to think straight.

"You're kidding?!" I said. "You mean to say that you've managed to miss Sunita?"

I stood up, my body felt sluggish. Every step I took seemed jerky, like an ultra-rapid film sequence. But I couldn't help feeling a glimmer of hope. Had they really missed Sunita? Was it even possible that they hadn't taken account of the greatest sadness in my life? Maybe there had been more mistakes.

"She broke my heart, for God's sake," I went on, in as reproachful a voice as I could muster. "That's affected my whole life. There's not a day goes by without me . . . I mean . . . Have you really not taken that into account?"

I could hear Maud's breathing speed up as she clicked between various documents.

"Er . . . Not as far as I can see."

"Holy shit," I said. "No wonder the invoice ended up being so expensive."

"When was this?" she asked.

I wondered if she was typing on her laptop. Had she logged in from bed? Or was she taking notes the old-fashioned way with pen and paper?

"1998," I said. "To 2000. January 5, 3.25p.m. We first met in '97, but didn't start seeing each other until the following year. Okay, hang on a minute, something like this has to be taken into account, even retrospectively, surely?"

I heard her moving at the other end.

"You're sure you're not getting mixed up with some film you've seen?"

"Are you kidding?" I said. "This is the biggest tragedy of my life."

She tapped at her computer again.

"But this has to be taken into consideration!" I said.

I was pacing up and down in the flat now.

"This could . . . Bloody hell!" I said.

She was breathing hard. I could tell things were serious this time.

"Yes. I think it would be best if you came back in again," she said.

CHAPTER
NINETEEN

On my second visit to W. R. D. a man came down and
met me in the vast entrance hall. Everyone seemed
extremely troubled by the mistake with Sunita. I was
assured that a thorough internal investigation would be
carried out, and led to believe that such occurrences
were extremely unusual, and that it must have
happened because she was a foreign citizen and the
relationship hadn't been registered anywhere, as well as
being kept secret from family and friends. Correspondence with their south Asian office hadn't been
entirely without friction, and the systems there
probably needed to be reconsidered. It had long been a
problematic area.

On the way out of the lift by the reception desk on
the eleventh floor I was met by an older woman in a
jacket and tight skirt, who made a rather girlish
impression in spite of her age. She smiled and tilted her
head as she spoke. She had a little scarf tied round
her neck, a bit like an air hostess. She thanked me for
my cooperation, and promised compensation for the
intrusion into my working hours. I didn't mention the
fact that I had simply swapped shifts with Tomas, who
wanted all the extra hours he could get before he went

off on holiday to Torremolinos. It was no problem at all. He had told me I could have the following day off too.

The woman in the scarf handed me an unwieldy bundle of forms, which she told me to fill in before the meeting. She led me through the open-plan office to the far end of the building, to another small room with glass walls. In one corner was a plant that looked like it was made of plastic. She pulled out a chair for me and asked if I'd like anything to drink while I went through the paperwork.

"I don't know," I said. "Some water, perhaps?"

"Still or sparkling?"

"Er . . . sparkling."

I sat down on the chair and began to fill in the forms.

The questions were concentrated around the years 1997 to 2002. I made a real effort to answer as truthfully as possible this time, and not exaggerate.

After a while the woman returned with a bottle of mineral water, a glass and a coaster. She put them down on the table a short distance from my papers.

"I'll be back shortly with a bottle-opener."

I thanked her and went on answering the questions as best I could.

It got quite warm in the little room when the sun came out, and I had to take off both my jacket and sweater and sit there in just my T-shirt. I checked a few times to see if I could smell sweat. It was much quieter in there than in the last meeting room — presumably at the expense of any ventilation. Every so often I looked around to see if I could catch a glimpse of Maud, but then I remembered that they had said something about her working down on the second floor. Anyway, I had no idea what she looked like. Even if I imagined that I'd know who she was as soon as I laid eyes on her.

The woman in the scarf stayed in the vicinity the whole time after she'd brought the bottle-opener. As soon as I was ready with one of the forms she would come in and get it. Otherwise she stayed outside the room. At one point Georg appeared and exchanged a few words with her. They both looked in my direction and I nodded slightly, but he showed no sign of returning my greeting.

After an hour or so inside the stuffy room I started to get tired. The questions were of various sorts: Describe an event. What happened first? What did you do next? Option 1, 2 or 3, and so on. There were various scales I had to make marks on. Circles and semicircles that I had to fill in or tick in the appropriate place. The questions kept probing into greater and greater detail. And into increasingly peripheral events. In the end my head was spinning and I was no longer sure if I was describing the truth or just a fantasy. How much of this had actually happened, and how much had I constructed in hindsight?

I tried to remember as many setbacks as possible. I made sure to give high points to anything related to pain and suffering.

Most of it was to do with my relationship with Sunita, but I also managed to squeeze in some of my and Roger's failed attempts to pick up girls.

110

Roger often dragged up "that disastrous night" many years ago when he and I had met Linda and Nicole. To him this was just more evidence of all the hardships he had to endure, but I wasn't sure if it ought to be regarded as entirely negative. We had been sitting in a bar and caught sight of two attractive girls a few tables away. We were both focused on the tall blonde with the incredibly pretty smile, whose name turned out to be Linda. During our discussion of tactics about who was going to go for which one, Roger argued that he should go for the blonde — the one we both liked most — because, as he put it, he deserved something nice for once. He thought I ought to be prepared to support him in this, and set my own sights on the brunette in the cap, and maybe even put in a good word for him so she could pass it on to her friend later.

I pointed out that it was a bit difficult to sort that out when we had no idea of their opinion on the matter, and that we should probably count ourselves lucky if they wanted to talk to us at all. Roger said I was just trying to make excuses, and in the end I agreed to try to set things up as best I could for him and the tall blonde.

After a couple of beers we plucked up the courage to go over to them, and luckily they asked us to sit down. I stuck to the agreement and mainly talked to Nicole, who turned out to work in comics and was great fun to talk to, while Roger and Linda had a separate conversation. All in all it was a very pleasant evening, and a couple of days later we started dating our respective girls.

I liked Nicole more and more. She taught me all about drawing and comics. She was very engaged with the environment and animal rights. She was a vegan too. Ate soya mince and You-can't-believe-it's-not-chicken, but occasionally her concentration would lapse. Sometimes she was halfway through a bag of sweets before realising that they contained gelatine. She would check the list of ingredients, then go and spit them out in the toilet. I enjoyed the afternoons and evenings I spent in her flat, lounging about on her sofa talking to her while she drew her cartoons. Sometimes she answered, sometimes she didn't. Sometimes she went off on long rants about society and Swedes and people in general. Her cartoons weren't all that nice to look at, or even particularly comprehensible. They weren't very realistic, but they were produced with passion and care. I loved them. We ended up getting it together, and went out for at least a month.

Roger and Linda embarked on a relationship as well, but I soon started to get reports about her failings. She talked too much, laughed too loudly, devoted too much time to her appearance. She was far too interested in his background. She would "interrogate" him, as he put it. Wanted to know what he thought about all sorts of things. She wanted to go out a lot too, and do fun things in the evenings, but these rarely turned out to be all that much fun, although they still cost a great deal of money. When she eventually — after Roger, on my suggestion, had told her that he wasn't comfortable doing all those expensive things and proposed that they stay at home and do things there instead — floated the idea that they experiment with more adventurous sex, he dumped her.

He came round to see me and Nicole and went on about how awful it was for him. He sat there on the sofa claiming that the world was against him.

"I was always going to end up with the nutter!" he said. "Typical. You had all the luck, as usual," he said to me, glaring at Nicole over at her drawing desk.

He also went into great detail explaining the difficulty he had had telling Linda that he didn't like cream in spray-cans, or blindfolds, and then — once he'd told her — finding a decent way to end it. He later declared that at least I hadn't had any of those problems, seeing as Nicole dumped me a few days later.

Once I'd described a number of occurrences with the help of an outline of the body on which you had to indicate where you felt your emotions were based, I had to fill in a load of forms with pre-printed questions where you had to rank different types of experience. Once again, they began with general issues and gradually became more specific.

I might have exaggerated slightly. Maybe I answered a little more negatively than I would have done under different circumstances.

For instance, in the column marked "Social Competence/further ed." I ticked the options connected to alienation, bullying and deficient group dynamics.

Under "Social Competence/dating/early rel./sex. exp." I took the opportunity to emphasise as much insecurity and performance anxiety as I could. They could probably work everything out themselves, down to the smallest detail, but I couldn't be entirely sure, seeing as they had missed the whole story of Sunita. Besides, I reasoned that it wouldn't do any harm if I added a bit of extra confusion with condoms and colliding front teeth.

Under "Work life/prev. empl." I ticked lots of boxes relating to irregular working hours, poor conditions and unpaid overtime.

When I was something like halfway through the pile of forms I went to the door and asked if I could have another bottle of water, but the woman in the scarf just shook her head. As if someone had told her not to leave her post on guard outside the glass box. I struggled through the rest of the questions and handed over the completed forms, by which time it was long past lunch.

"Can I go now?" I asked.

"No," she said, looking rather excited. "You have to come with me."

She led the way to the reception desk and left my forms there. I sat down in the same armchair as before, and the woman in the scarf went and stood by the lift. A few moments later Georg emerged from the frosted-glass door. He went over to the desk, collected my bundle of papers, then disappeared into the secret room again. The woman and I were left in reception.

She must have stood there by the lift for two hours while I tried to find a comfortable position in the narrow armchair. I stretched out as far as I could, but it was obvious the chair wasn't made for long-term use. I felt tired and sweaty and a bit dazed after all those

114

questionnaires. There were posters on the wall next to the lift, and the table in front of me was covered with all sorts of information leaflets from the campaign I had evidently missed. "Time to pay — have you checked your E. H. score?", "Give or take?", "Time to even things out!", in large, slanting blue lettering printed over colourful pictures of children and adults. They were in a number of different languages. As I looked at them, it dawned on me that I may well have seen those leaflets at home somewhere, but had thrown them in the recycling without ever thinking that they concerned me. They looked disconcertingly similar to all the other advertisements that I usually ignored. I picked up one of the brochures and leafed through it. There was a short history, and an account of the big international agreement. Various politicians and leaders from different areas of society were quoted: short, punchy sentences.

It went on to give a description of the next step: the process of redistribution, when those with negative scores were going to receive compensation, and how this was going to happen. Towards the end were contact details for anyone wanting to lodge a complaint or who thought they had been unjustly treated.

From time to time, as I sat there reading, people went up to the reception desk. Some had similar questions to mine. Some wanted more detailed repayment proposals, some were angry. Some came to plead their case, others swore and gesticulated wildly. I wondered if my amount was higher or lower than the average.

A couple of times I almost dozed off, and once I was roused by a voice that seemed strangely familiar. After a while I realised that it was the girl with the necklaces from the lift in my building, the one whose phone call I had overheard a few days before, standing and talking over at the desk. She seemed really on top of things as she spoke to the receptionist. She took out some papers and a loan agreement, and explained the repayment schedule she had worked out for herself. I couldn't help but be a bit impressed by her proactive attitude. I was struck by the advantage people like that had in society. She was probably already saving for her retirement, compared electricity suppliers, and had registered her children — born or unborn — for the best schools. And now she was here to get the lowest interest rate possible. For a moment I felt a little envious, and thought that I ought to be more like her. The sort of person who could look after themselves and sort things out. Then I would probably never have ended up in this situation. As it was, I had to stake everything on Sunita.

Eventually the woman with the bank-name appeared.

"Hello! We've met before, of course," she said, and it occurred to me that it wouldn't be a good idea to ask for her name again, so I was none the wiser this time. She was dressed in a mauve jacket and skirt, the same severe cut as before, but now she had a large artificial violet-coloured flower attached to her lapel. She was holding a folder to her chest, and led me into the big conference room. She asked me to take a seat. The woman in the scarf stayed outside.

116

Shortly afterwards Georg arrived, bringing with him an older man with bushy eyebrows and a dimpled chin. The three of them stood in a little group on the other side of the table, and the woman with the bank-name gave the new arrival a brief summary of my case. Every so often Georg interrupted with a clarification. Sometimes they very nearly talked at once. I recognised some of the terminology this time.

"Maximal E. H. score . . ."

"High values for euphoria, harmony, sorrow and pain, melancholy . . ."

"Sensitivity?"

"Maximal, as far as we can tell. But without lasting trauma . . . and, well, you know what that means. The resulting experiential charge shoots up . . ."

The woman held up a graph that the other two studied very carefully.

"Bloody hell, that's the highest quotient," the man with the eyebrows said.

"Definitely. I've got nothing but fives here . . ."

They bent over another document.

"And the curve for shortcomings?"

"Latent," she said.

"To take one example, he's only declared life-enhancing humiliation," Georg said. "Nothing but character-forming setbacks. All according to the progression framework. There's no deviation from the development model. He's almost a textbook example of the *Live for today* template."

"The only infections he's suffered occurred at exactly the right time to cause the least possible problems and

117

the mildest symptoms, yet with optimal results for his immune system. Just look at this graph . . ."

They lowered their voices and I could only hear fragments of what they were saying, because they were trying not to be overheard. Occasionally they covered their mouths with their hands.

". . . almost absurd levels of pleasure . . . And full access to his feelings. According to our contact, on certain occasions the subject has the ability to forget basic simplifying acts in daily life which on sudden recollection give a two-fold increase to his E. H."

"And now . . ." the woman with the bank-name said, picking up a new folder. "Now a hitherto unknown relation-ship has come to light. With a woman named Sunita."

"Look here," Georg said, pointing with his pen at the new folder. "Post-Sunita, life-affirming results all the way." He leafed forward a few pages and pointed again. "Here again . . . life-affirming."

The others nodded.

"Excuse me," I said.

All three of them looked at me, aghast. As if they'd forgotten I was sitting there, or didn't know I could talk.

"I thought I was going to be seeing Maud," I went on.

The man with the eyebrows looked quizzically at the woman with the bank-name.

"Maud?" he said. "Who's this Maud?"

"Maud Andersson," she replied. "Apparently she works down on the second floor. He has indicated . . ."

She turned to a different page.

". . . here that he thinks 'She is doing a very good job.'"

118

The eyebrows were suddenly fixed on me.

"I see," he said, shaking his head at me. "No," he said. "No, no, it will just be the three of us."

He put one hand to his mouth as he leafed through the file with the other.

"Intellect?" he muttered to the woman.

"Intact," she replied.

"Here again," Georg said, still looking down at the file. "Look, same as before . . ."

As I sat there watching these three people my attention was taken by the new man's build. His body looked out of proportion. At first I couldn't work out what it was, then I realised that his legs were far too short. Which meant that he had an extremely low waist. The end result was about right. He was more or less of normal height, but now that I came to think about it he was almost entirely torso. It looked a bit odd when you saw them standing next to each other.

The woman with the bank-name took out another diagram. Georg interjected from the other side: "We can't possibly allow continued access as things stand," he said.

"No," the man with the torso whispered. "He's past the debt ceiling, so we'll have to impose a 6:3 on him."

The others reacted sharply.

"A 6:3?"

One of them took out another document. The meeting moved further along the table as the paperwork spread out. They slowly sat down as they carried on talking.

"He can't request any deductions either," the woman said. "He hasn't really had any grounds on each of the . . ." She fell silent for a moment. Almost as if she had lost her train of thought.

As if on a given signal, all three stopped and looked over at me. Astonished.

I realised that I was something special. Georg broke the silence.

"But," he began slowly, "as I understand it, his repayment capacity is practically zero?"

The woman and Georg took turns tapping new numbers into a calculator.

The man with the bushy eyebrows and short legs was still staring at me. He very slowly leaned across the table and held out his hand, as if it had only just occurred to him that he ought to shake my hand. I took hold of it, and he pressed my hand, at the same time as continuing his conversation with the other two.

"Have we carried out a home inventory?" he said, still not taking his eyes off me. As if the handshake was taking place in a parallel world.

Georg and the woman both shook their heads. The man with the eyebrows replied with a low rumble of disapproval.

"See that it gets done as soon as possible."

He leaned back and sat down on his chair again.

"Well . . . ," he said, looking through the file until he found my name. Then, when he evidently realised it was too late to get personal, he didn't bother to say it. He simply nodded, as if he were content merely to know what my name was.

"Your debt has just been increased to 149,500,000 kronor."

CHAPTER
TWENTY

The inspectors came early the next day. I opened the door and let them into the flat just after half past seven in the morning. They were large and taciturn. Careful and thorough. They worked efficiently and almost without speaking to each other. They went through my belongings quickly and methodically, rather like customers officers. A woman in the same sort of uniform looked through my clothes and registered the things in the bathroom. I tried to help them as much as I could, but soon realised that they were best left to their own devices.

For each item they made a small mark in a pad. They pulled out my kitchen drawers, opened my cupboards. Checked my pictures and photographs. They dealt with some things in bulk. One of the men looked at only a couple of my vinyl record collection, for instance. And not even the two most valuable. None of them noticed my copy of Jimmy Smith's *Softly as a Summer Breeze*, for example, no scratches, original pressing. The one checking the records merely shook his head and made a note.

An hour later they were finished. One of them handed me a "next-of-kin form" that he said I should fill in. They thanked me and left.

I sat on the floor looking at my things. Now that the men had gone, they felt even more worthless.

It was oppressively hot inside the flat. The kind of sticky heat that clung to your body. Like having a tight helmet round your brain. It was as bad as trying to breathe in a sauna, and it didn't get any better when I opened the windows even wider. The sultry air outside was completely still. Swallows were flying low. I looked at the piece of paper in my hand and wondered who I should give as my next-of-kin. Jörgen? Roger? In the end I wrote my sister's name and address.

I paced up and down in my boiling-hot living room and tried to make sense of my thoughts. Had I presented everything wrong? Was there something I'd missed? Was it really possible to claim, as W. R. D. were, that I had taken the best from my relationship with Sunita? Okay, so our relationship was already starting to feel a bit tired when we separated. We didn't really share any interests beyond film, and we didn't agree on most things. She had a rather spoiled way of looking at the world, but at the same time she could seem pretty helpless. She was provocatively uninterested in other cultures, and declared on one occasion when we were having a row that I was more or less insignificant. That what we had together was only a parenthesis, something that didn't count, and, quite regardless of what she might feel now, would have absolutely no impact on her future. It was as if she didn't really value her own feelings. As if everything she had with me, all the films and her education, our entire culture, was just one long dream. Soon enough she would be going back to reality. She was Daddy's little princess, and when I once pointed out that he didn't seem to have been in touch for several years it was enough to make her expression freeze and break the spell between us.

It wasn't that great standing outside in the winter and shivering in different places, waiting for a sign that might or might not come. Towards the end she had almost seemed a bit bored, as if she had had enough. I dare say we both realised that it wouldn't have lasted much longer, but the fact that we were forced to split up suddenly made the whole thing feel incredibly sad. And the pain. The pain! I could still feel it as I walked about sweating between the window and the living-room table.

As soon as I'd pulled myself together I called Maud again. At first I couldn't get through to her. They said she was busy, and had therefore redirected her calls to reception. Did I want to leave a message?

I said I needed to talk to her, and that it was urgent, and I must have sounded persistent and difficult and aggressive enough, because in the end they put me through anyway.

"So, are you done with me now, then?" I said.

"I don't know," she said. "Have you got anything else sensational to report?"

I yelled that this was completely unreasonable, and how the hell did they actually work things out? But Maud managed to stay calm and said that I was the one who had withheld information. I begged and pleaded and shouted in turn. I wondered how the business with Sunita could *increase* my debt when it ought to have done the reverse. For the first time she sounded tense and rather nervous. I realised that she was under pressure. Perhaps because of all the miscalculations and mistakes. She said I shouldn't think I could judge things like this better than some of the country's most prominent experts and psychiatrists and psychologists, the people who had developed the system.

After a while I calmed down and felt stupid. After all, it wasn't her fault that things were the way they were.

"How serious is it?" I asked after a brief pause.

"Well," she said, and even though she was making a real effort to sound calm, I could tell that she was upset. "You should have told me about Sunita . . ."

"I assumed you already knew —"

She interrupted me before I could finish, and sounded very apologetic.

"Of course, that was our fault," she said. "I don't understand how we could have missed such a . . ."

"So what happens now?"

"I don't know. You're now registered as a so-called 6:3, and I can tell you that you've already gone through the debt ceiling . . ."

I got up from the floor, waving the next-of-kin form in my hand. I was breathing hard down the phone.

"But . . . we were going to sort this out . . ."

She didn't let me finish.

"That was before Sunita," she said. "And from what you told us, that only raises the credit side."

124

"How can it do that?" I said. "It was one of the worst experiences of my life . . ."

"The way you described it, you had a fantastic time."

I noticed that I was shouting again. "Until she was snatched away from me! We were forced to . . . well, separate, under extremely . . . extremely painful circumstances. How can that be counted as something positive?"

She snapped back at me.

"Come off it!" she hissed. "It's pure Hollywood! How many people do you think . . .?"

Her voice was almost trembling. She fell silent for a moment, as if to compose herself, but soon carried on.

"How many people do you think experience anything like that? Ever? Anywhere?"

She tried to revert to cooler, more formal vocabulary, but her tone of voice gave her away. "And you still had your self-esteem intact at the end. According to your declaration, you could have drawn the experience out . . . so to speak . . . even after the conclusion of the relationship involving physical contact."

She flared up again. Sounded properly angry for the first time. Almost as if she were lecturing me.

"And you tried to make out that your life was more or less a waste of time? Well? Isn't that what you did? Wasn't that the whole point of your last phone call? I almost fell for it. You're actually a perversely happy person!"

I didn't say anything at first. Then I mumbled something about unfair calculations and other more

125

successful people around me, but Maud dismissed all my objections.

"It's not as simple as that. You understand that, surely? It's impossible to make generalisations . . . It's all about the combination . . . and your specific combination of experiences in life has turned out to be extremely happy."

"Fine! What about everyone else, then?" I exclaimed.

For a moment there was total silence. It was like she was thinking hard.

"You really don't get it, do you?" she eventually said.

"What?" I said.

Quiet now. Almost a whisper.

"People are extremely unhappy. Most people feel really bad! They're in pain. They're poor, sick, on medication, depressed, scared, worried about all sorts of things. They're stressed and panicked, they feel guilty, suffer performance anxiety, have trouble sleeping, can't concentrate, or they're just bored, or constantly under pressure, or feel that they're being treated badly. Deceived, unsuccessful, guilty — anything and everything. At most, the majority of people experience a few years of relative happiness in their childhood. That's often when they build up their score. After that it's pretty bleak."

She sighed, making the line crackle, and I thought I could hear her shake her head.

"If only you knew," she said.

I sat down against the wall again. She took a deep breath and went on: "You see, we look at life as if it were a classically constructed play. The one with the most whistles and bells isn't necessarily the best. Things

126

have to happen in the right order, too, otherwise there's no point . . ."

I realised I'd never heard Maud talk like this before. And I recognised that there was a sort of trust, an honesty between us that it would be hard to manage without now that these conversations were drawing to a natural conclusion. Because even if I was upset about the way things were, I really didn't want anything else but to sit and talk to her on the phone. Talking about stuff. Listening to her voice. But I said nothing. I realised that it would hardly work in my favour.

I could hear her rustle some paper again. For the first time I suspected that she was doing it to make it sound as if she had more important things to be getting on with. Maybe she just did it when she couldn't think of anything to say.

"So . . ." she said after a pause. "That film, what was it called? I watched it."

She fell silent, but I couldn't hear any paper rustling this time.

"*The Bridge?*" I said. "You watched *The Bridge?*"

She sighed. And once again that strange warm feeling spread through me. She had taken the time to get hold of a Bosnian film from the turn of the millennium for the simple reason that I had recommended it.

"I rented it," she said. "And that scene you talked about. The one in the café. It was, well, I don't know how to put it . . ."

"You rented *The Bridge?* How did you manage to get hold of it?"

"I got hold of it, okay?!" she said irritably. "So I sat down and watched it. I waited for that scene, and it eventually came. But, well, there was none of that stuff you were going on about. It was just two people sitting there. In a café. So what? It was pretty boring. Terrible lighting."

"Oh, come on," I began. "No, I don't think that's —"

"Don't you get it?" she said. "You're the one who read all those looks and touches and everything into it," she said. "They're all in your head."

I stood up and went over to the window.

"No, I don't think . . ."

She went on: "But I ought to have realised that by now. It's typical of you. You think you're discovering a whole load of things, but they aren't really there. No wonder you got such a high E. H. score."

"But they touched each other," I said. "You must have seen them touch each other!"

"It's all one single scene, no editing. The camera's a long way away. The whole time. It was all done in one take. You can hardly see anything."

"Okay, but *that's* what's so . . ."

"Sure, they put their arms next to each other, but that's all there was to it."

I tried to find the right words.

"Yeah, but you still understand . . ."

"What is it you understand?" she said. "*What?*"

"Their little fingers touch . . ."

"Yes, but what is it you understand?"

"You see how —"

"What do you see? You could hardly even see their hands. What's so special about it? Grainy and black-and-white and all in long-shot. To me it was just an endlessly drawn-out scene where practically nothing happened."

"How can you say that?" I said. "It's completely magical . . ."

"It's impossible to tell from that distance. If they'd filmed a bit closer, maybe, but it was just one single, drawn-out shot."

I really wanted to say something, but couldn't get the words out.

"No," she said, and this time I'm sure I could hear her shake her head. "You filled in all those details for yourself."

"But all great art . . ." I began.

"It's brilliant that you can extract so much emotion from that scene, but I have to look at it practically," she said. "To me it was just unbearably dull."

The two of us said nothing for a long time. The only sound was the noise of her colleagues in the background. The next-of-kin form in my hand was damp and crumpled now.

"If I could just watch that scene with you . . ." I said.

"You won't have time to watch anything," she said. "They're probably already on their way to you now."

"What? Who . . .?" I said. "What's going on now?"

She took a deep breath and began speaking in a low, confidential voice so that no one else in the office would hear her, as if she were telling me something I really shouldn't know.

129

"You're about to be picked up by one of your teams —"

"Picked up?" I exclaimed.

"Shhh! Yes, what did you expect? You can't possibly have further access under the circumstances."

I could definitely hear emotion in her voice now. Even though she was really trying to sound businesslike.

"There's nothing I can do as things stand . . ."

I let the phone slip slowly down my cheek, until it hit my shoulder and fell to the floor. I heard her call my name from down there several times.

CHAPTER
TWENTY-ONE

Clouds were gathering outside. Big, lead-grey billows were rolling in over the rooftops. The sun passed behind them and soon there was a flash of lightning, like a momentary camera-flash lighting up the whole city. There was a thunderous rumble and the first heavy drops were in the air. Soon the rain was pattering on the window sill and bouncing in onto the floor. I should have shut the windows, but I just sat there paralysed, staring at the cloud of dancing droplets.

What did she mean by "picked up"? What did "no further access" mean? In my mind's eye I saw myself being segregated, with one of those cones you put on dogs, to stop me absorbing any more experiences. Light, sound, birds, wind, all the things I liked, even rain and stormy weather. I tried to think of really dull days, but suddenly everything seemed so wonderful. I really did try to imagine a properly grey day, but without meaning to I found myself thinking of water gushing out of the bottom of a drainpipe. So wet. The water in general. The whole principle of water. What the air is like when it rains. Drops against my skin. Girls I'd seen out in the rain. The way their clothes stuck to their skin, and that film, *The Umbrellas of Cherbourg*, which Sunita had made me watch, and which I honestly hadn't appreciated at all until afterwards, in hindsight, when she was gone. When all I had left were the things she opened my eyes to. A whole load of things that I now loved. The measured pace of Rachmaninoff's sonata for cello and piano, for instance. Bloody hell — there was no escape!

I shook my head and tried to conjure up images of terrible monsters and horrible demons. I tried to make them as vicious and dangerous as possible, but no matter how hard I thought of tails and tongues and teeth, they never ended up as anything but colourful characters in a computer game. I looked round the room in an attempt to find something really grim, tragic, or at least depressing, but everything I could see felt secure and beautiful and held only happy associations. My beloved old sofa, my lovely cushions, the wonderful poster of M. C. Escher's perfectly mathematical illusion. The damp, and the tiny drops of the liberating, oxygen-rich rain that occasionally reached the tops of my arms . . . I was still hopelessly happy.

For the first time I was struck by the unsettling thought that the true value of my Experienced Happiness might have actually been seriously undervalued.

CHAPTER
TWENTY-TWO

Ten minutes later, when the men from W. R. D. knocked on the door, I was still sitting there, leaning against the wall in the same position. I had just thought of a summer some years ago when I'd borrowed Lena and Fredrik's cottage. At first I felt a bit lonely, but as the days passed I felt more and more liberated. And weightless. In the end I stopped noticing the passage of time, and even forgot how old I was. I would cycle slowly down to the lake through warm, gentle summer rain, and I was all ages at the same time. I got to my feet and went to open the door.

They said hello politely and waited for me to go to the toilet and get changed before we headed off to the vast granite complex, where we drove down into a large garage. We got out and went up in the lift to the same reception area where I had been twice before. Rain was lashing the big windows, sounding like hundreds of little drums.

Georg met us at the desk. He nodded to the guards and indicated that they could go now. This time he had with him two very well-dressed foreign gentlemen who didn't speak Swedish. He introduced them in English, and I was told that they were from head office in

Toronto, and the Calgary subsidiary. They smiled at me and seemed pleasant enough. Neither of them said much. They mostly fiddled with their phones while we waited. I couldn't help wondering what was going to happen.

I held the next-of-kin form out to Georg, who looked at it with surprise and hesitantly took it.

"Of course, yes, this . . ." he said slowly. "I don't really know who . . . This is really just a trial, so far . . ."

After a while another man came and got the two foreign men. Georg remained standing over by the desk and I sat down in an armchairwhile the others disappeared into the conference room with the noisy ventilation. He looked at my form for a while, then put it down on the desk beside him.

"Well, then." He sighed, and shook his head.

He sat down in the chair next to me and gave me a sympathetic look. I realised I was sweating. I looked round to see if I could see any handcuffs, or a cage, or anything like that.

"What are you going to do?" I asked in as relaxed a voice as possible.

He shook his head.

"No," he said. "I'm not going to pre-empt anything, but it doesn't look good. Not good at all . . ."

Everyone who walked past looked completely normal, and seemed preoccupied with their own concerns. No one looked at me oddly, so I assumed that only a small group there at W. R. D. knew about my situation and what was likely to happen to me.

I was having trouble sitting still. I turned round and tried to look into the glass office where meetings were usually held, and where a large number of people were now leaning over something on the table. Some of them were gesticulating with their arms. It was like they were waiting for a particular signal, or perhaps another participant. I took a deep breath and tried to stop my hands shaking on my lap.

"Why me?" I asked Georg, almost in a whisper.

He shrugged his shoulders. As if it was a question that couldn't possibly be answered easily.

"What about all the millionaires?"

He smiled and ran his hand through the hair that may or may not have been dyed.

"Believe me, we're taking care of them as well. Most wealthy people will obviously receive a fairly hefty invoice. But it isn't always so simple. To take just one example, let me tell you about . . . hmm, let's call him Kjell."

He sat up in his chair and leaned towards me.

"Kjell worked at a factory in Stegsta and lived a quiet life in all respects. He mostly kept to himself. He did his job, saved some money, and was eventually offered the chance to buy some shares in Stegsta Ltd, which shot up in value shortly afterwards. Two or three years later they were worth five times what Kjell had paid, and he sold the shares at an impressive profit. He ended up with a small fortune, which he looked after carefully, whilst still going to work as usual. Each year his capital grew in various funds and investment accounts. When I asked if he wasn't thinking of doing

135

something fun with the money, he always said he was planning to take early retirement and have his fun then. I couldn't help thinking that if anyone had the strength of character to do that, it was Kjell. Sure enough, he retired at the age of fifty-five. The day after he left work he called and said triumphantly: 'At last, I'm free!'

"I didn't hear from him for six months. There was nothing unusual about that. He wasn't the sociable type and I assumed he was in the Bahamas or on some luxury cruise or whatever someone with plenty of time and money might come up with. But the next time he called he was in an acute psychiatric treatment centre.

"He had ended up having severe anxiety attacks. He was depressed, but not just feeling a bit low and thinking that life was a bit miserable. He was depressed in a way that didn't mean finding new ways to think about things or to get going with his life again, or eating better and enjoying the little things, nothing like that. For him it was about whether he could be bothered to get out of bed in the morning. And not give up and put an end to it all. It was about deciding at each moment to go on living. Resisting the easy option for one more day, one more hour, one more minute. He said when it was at its worst, he just sat there breathing and looking at the time. Waiting for the relapse into darkness to pass."

Georg leaned back again.

"The E. H. score he had gained because of his financial success fell away, like cherry blossom in May, when there was no longer anything to push against."

He looked at me to see if I'd understood.

136

"Naturally there are special cases," I said. "But what about all the others? The ones whose lives are a never-ending party. The ones with loads of friends and acquaintances. Fast cars. Lovers. I haven't got anything like that."

"A large social circle can be a good thing, of course," he went on. "And lots of parties. But it's the quality that's important. Too many contacts can lead to stress — it actually reduces E. H. scores. Increased financial assets also raise expectations. And some things that at first glance can look like negatives actually end up raising the score dramatically. Take your own case, for instance, and everything connected to pain and pleasure. How do you think we deal with the BDSM community?"

He raised his eyebrows. I couldn't think of anything to say.

"Children, then?" I said after a while. "I haven't got children. And that must be the meaning of everything to some extent . . ."

He sighed and rubbed one eye with a finger.

"You keep picking out individual things. None of them need necessarily mean anything by itself. There's no such thing as an unambiguously positive event. Or an isolated state of happiness. Besides, I seem to recall that your sister has children . . .?"

I shook my head and sighed.

"You're very smart," I said.

He laughed and looked at me. And held up his hands in a way that said, *I rest my case*.

137

"You see," Georg said, "that way you have of being impressed by everything you experience. In our formulas . . . well, what can I say? It quickly mounts up."

"I've always been so cautious," I muttered, slowly shaking my head. "I've never really pushed for anything . . ."

He looked at me as if he wondered what I was getting at. As if he couldn't really work out if I was actually heading somewhere with my argument, or just drifting about aimlessly in an attempt to gain time.

"Yes," he said, "there are advantages and disadvantages to everything. But in your case . . . well, it certainly looks as if the advantages have the upper hand."

He looked me in the eye again.

"You must realise that very few people even come close to a score like yours?"

I nodded and looked over at the window, where the rain was forming thick lines on the glass. Like little rivers. He narrowed his eyes slightly.

"You've maintained a very constant level," he said. "And with so little personal effort. It's very odd. Fascinating, actually."

"I suppose so," I said. "It's just that I probably expected . . ."

"What?" he said. "What did you expect?"

He fixed his eyes on me.

"More?" he suggested.

I squirmed.

"There must be people who have lived — how can I put it? — far more passionately. People who've followed their desires. I don't know. Fucking around. Taking drugs."

"Most narcotics also have drawbacks," he said bluntly. "I presume you know that."

I nodded.

"That's also a typical masculine trait," he said. "Men always assume that more money means more happiness."

"Really?" I said. "Still . . . a friend of mine . . ."

He shook his head dismissively.

"Let's not start making comparisons."

"I know. But we did," I said. "And the woman who . . . Well, I happened to find out how much she was being charged, and it seems quite unreasonable that she should have such a lower amount than me."

"Like I said . . ."

"I just don't get it," I said.

He folded his arms.

"What does your friend do?"

"She works h . . . I mean . . . She . . . she has a similar job to you . . ."

Just as I was thinking that I mustn't give anything away with my body language, I realised that I'd already glanced over at the conference room. He looked at me. He suddenly became very serious. He was silent for several long moments, studying me without blinking.

"I don't mean what job she has," he said slowly, also glancing over at the glass-walled room containing the others. "I mean, what does she *do*? How does she act? How does she pass her time, and how is that connected to her well-being?"

"Oh," I said hesitantly. "Well, I don't really know her like that . . ."

"No," he said quickly, and leaned closer to me again. "You've got no idea, have you? You don't know what psycho-social effect her work could have on her, for instance. Or how many negative interactions she may have in her life."

I shook my head and tried to find the right words.

"She . . . well, she doesn't seem depressed," I said. "We get on pretty well, actually . . ."

He wasn't listening to me, and went on: "And you don't know anything about her daily life, about the depersonalising impact of her work. And do you know what?"

He moved closer to me and lowered his voice to a whisper.

"If I were you," he said, "I'd keep very quiet about this 'friend'."

He looked over at the meeting room, where the others were preparing for my arrival.

"If only for her sake . . ."

The man who had shown the foreign gentlemen in some time ago was suddenly standing next to me.

"We're ready," he said. "You can come in now."

I turned round and felt my pulse speed up. Georg was already on his feet, and I was about to stand up when I realised that I had to take my chance. Who knew if there would be any more chances at all? I leaned back.

"I want Maud to be here," I said.

140

They both stopped and looked at me.

"Maud?" the man said. "Who's Maud?"

"Maud Andersson," I said.

He looked round.

"There's no Maud here," he said.

"Yes, there is," I said. "Maud Andersson. I want her here."

Georg turned to the new man.

"She works on the second floor, apparently," he said. "She's been his contact here."

"Oh?" the man said uninterestedly, as if he were wondering how this could change anything.

"You could get them to call down and see if she's there," Georg said.

"Yes, do that," I said. "I'll wait here."

The new man stood there for a moment looking at me, then he went over to the desk and spoke to the receptionist.

Georg sat down again and looked at me. After a while he leaned over.

"A little tip," he said. "If it turns out that your 'friend' here has interacted with you in an inappropriate way, it may well be that we won't be able to retain her services. Do you understand? I can't imagine that you want that. You want her to keep her job, don't you?"

I think I nodded. He leaned back in his chair. We sat there in silence for a while.

Eventually the new man returned.

"She's on her way up," he said.

CHAPTER
TWENTY-THREE

This time there were four of them. Plus the two foreign gentlemen. Another man, slightly overweight and with very little hair, just some above his ears, had taken a seat at one side of the table, where a number of documents relating to my case had been laid out. I sat down on the same chair as the previous two occasions.

The bald, thickset man introduced himself as Pierre, and he must have been superior to all the others, because whenever he spoke they all listened breathlessly. He frowned and fixed his eyes on me. He sat there for a long time just staring at me.

"I hear you've had a decent life?"

I nodded.

"Without paying your way."

I nodded again. He called the two foreigners over to him. He pointed at something in the documents, and the other two men raised their eyebrows. One of them let out a whistle. "Wow," the other one said, and nodded appreciatively in my direction. When they had returned to their seats, Pierre turned back to me.

"And you've built up quite a sizeable debt," he said.

There was a modest knock on the door.

And there she was at last.

★　★　★

Outside the glass stood a woman with dark blonde hair in a ponytail. She was wearing a black polo-necked top and a jacket with plenty of practical little pockets. A dark corduroy skirt and black tights. She had her arms clasped in front of her stomach, her hands clutching the handle of a briefcase. They opened the door for her and she took a couple of steps into the room, nodded to her colleagues, and when Georg went over to say hello I saw her straighten up and almost stand on tiptoe, so that the heels of her matt black shoes with white buckles lifted slightly off the ground.

She turned towards me. I found myself getting to my feet.

Georg indicated a chair next to mine. She walked towards me, put the briefcase in one hand and held the other one out to me.

"What's this person doing here?" Pierre hissed to the woman with the bank-name.

"She's his contact here," she said. "He's requested that she be here."

Pierre looked sceptically from Maud to me.

"Really?" he mumbled.

"Maud," she said quietly, and I realised that I was smiling as I heard her voice. She was smiling as well. It was like she was smiling at my smile, and I at hers, then she was smiling back at mine a bit more, and so on, ad infinitum. The smile revealed a neat but slightly irregular row of teeth. One of them was crooked and seemed to be winking at me as she smiled at me. A

143

short curl of hair that wasn't tied up hung down one side of her face, and looked as if it was gently tickling her soft, slightly blushing cheeks whenever she moved her head. She smelled vaguely of coffee and deodorant.

"Nice to meet you," she said to me.

"Same here," I said.

She had a small necklace outside the wonderful polo-necked sweater, I guessed it was probably half cotton, half polyester. The necklace had what looked like a silver dolphin on it, but it could have been any fish really. The skin just under her chin moved slightly when she spoke. It looked soft, smooth. I wanted to touch it.

"So," Pierre said. "Are we all ready, then?"

He tapped his pen impatiently on the tabletop, evidently extremely put out by the small delay. He pursed his lips silently as he waited for Maud to take her place beside me. She put her briefcase down on the floor next to her chair, took out a pen and notepad, and did a quick scribble in one corner to check that the pen was working.

"As I was saying," Pierre said to me as soon as she was ready, "you've built up a fairly sizeable debt, to put it mildly."

He looked round the room.

"You are now what we call a 6:3. For that reason we have conducted a home inventory, which came up with . . . nothing."

He gestured lazily towards one of the documents on the table, it was impossible to tell which one.

"Absolutely nothing," he said to the gentlemen at the other end of the table, and to make his point even more clearly he addressed me in a rather loud voice and with exaggerated pronunciation: "You own nothing of value."

I wasn't sure how to respond, so I just nodded slightly to indicate that I'd heard what he said.

"No education, so no immediate prospect of increased earnings . . ."

"If I don't win the lottery," I said, in a nervous attempt at a joke.

I looked at Maud, who registered no reaction.

Pierre gave a supercilious smile and adopted my tone.

"Quite. And of course we can't kill you," he said.

He smiled towards the foreign representatives, and they smiled back. All of a sudden I became aware that my palms were sweating. He leaned across the table towards me.

"Are there any more people you've socialised with but not declared?" he said.

I shook my head.

"You're sure about that?"

I couldn't help glancing at Maud, who was looking straight ahead the whole time.

"Not as far as I'm aware," I said. "Is it important?"

Pierre maintained eye contact the whole time he spoke. As if he really did want to see how I reacted to what he said.

"With this type of positive perception, there's reason to suppose that people in the immediate vicinity will register a certain — how can I put it? — passive gain. It could raise their E. H. score dramatically. After their cases have been re-evaluated, of course."

I noticed that one of the surveillance cameras up at the ceiling suddenly moved slightly. Presumably there were even more people watching us. Maybe via direct streaming to other countries?

He sat and fiddled with his pen for a while. Suddenly he clapped his hands together, and gestured to the other people in the room, who all stood up. Then he turned to Maud.

"Would you please stay here with the subject while we have a short meeting in private?" he said.

Maud nodded.

They all walked out, leaving just the two of us alone in the room. As soon as they had gone I turned to face her, but she quickly cleared her throat and glanced up at one of the cameras as if to remind me that we were probably still being observed, and that this wasn't a place where we could talk freely. So I turned back and we sat there in silence, next to one another, like passengers on a train, listening to the sound of the ventilation in the ceiling.

After a while she put one arm on the table to adjust one of the documents. The sleeve of her jacket had slid up towards her elbow, so most of her lower arm was lying bare on the table, right next to me. I waited a while, maybe thirty seconds, before putting my arm alongside hers. Not close, but not too far away.

We sat like that for a bit. Nothing happened. Maud leafed through the papers in front of her with her other hand, and I understood how the rustling sound I had

146

heard over the phone was made. She would fold back a few pages to check something, then let them go again before checking something else. All with the same hand. The arm next to mine remained still. We could both hear the discussions taking place outside. Several voices, in a number of different languages. It wasn't possible to see any of the people speaking, but it sounded as if more or less the whole department was involved in the same noisy conversation. Only inside the room containing Maud and me was everything calm and still.

Eventually she pushed one of the documents closer to me, and the arm nearest to me joined in. We were now very close. I took a deep breath and turned my hand over, so that the back of it touched the back of her hand. At that precise moment she stopped and remained absolutely still. There was nothing but the voices outside, the faint drumming of the rain, and the dust drifting slowly through the air. Neither of us said anything. We kept looking forward, into the frosted-glass wall in front of us, as if there was actually something interesting to see there. And then a tiny movement, barely visible to the naked eye, and absolutely impossible to detect from a surveillance camera up by the ceiling, for instance, as her little finger slowly touched the back of my hand, and our breathing synchronised in the same rhythm.

The doors opened and the delegation came back into the room. Our hands moved apart as quickly and silently as they had come together. Everyone but Pierre

147

went back to their previous places. Pierre folded his arms and wandered up and down along the side of the table. When he had done this a couple of times he sat down opposite us and smiled at Maud. Then he looked at me and his smile died away.

"Sorry to make you wait," he said, then took a deep breath and slowly blew the air out again, as he leaned forward and clasped his hands together above the table. He rested his chin on the knuckles, and sat like that for a while just looking at me, waiting for all movement in the room to stop before he resumed speaking in a calm, confidential tone of voice.

"You see, we are faced with an extremely costly investment which would appear to stand very little chance of collecting any significant repayment."

He looked around the table at the others before his eyes settled on me again.

"Naturally we could carry on and impose further . . . but I can't really see that that would be worthwhile . . . can you?"

I nodded. It seemed best to agree with him.

"Unless," he went on in a more light-hearted tone, "you see any possibility of promotion at, er . . . 'Jugge's Flicks'?"

I shook my head. He smiled, but his eyes remained cold.

"No, I thought as much," he said.

He closed his eyes for a moment, as if he were trying to work out how to phrase something. Then he snapped them open again and looked straight at me.

148

"The cost of keeping you isolated — and yes, I see here that you have an ability, even in the most trying of circumstances, to maintain a certain, how can I put it . . .?"

His eyes flitted about, trying to find a particular document. The woman with the bank-name and the others hurried to find the right one, but when they eventually found it and put it in front of him, he waved it away and went on staring at me.

"You know what people say: if you owe the bank a million, it's your problem, but if you owe a hundred million . . ."

I nodded. Yes, I'd heard that one. He lowered his voice even more and sharpened his tone. Everyone in the room held their breath.

"So what I'm going to suggest must stay between us. Do you understand? Under no circumstances must this get out."

He fixed his eyes on me and I wasn't sure if I'd stopped nodding from last time, so I nodded extra hard to show that I was keeping up.

Without looking away from me, he gestured to a woman outside who, with some help, pushed a wheeled trolley into the room. On top of the trolley was a pile of papers twenty centimetres thick.

"Please be aware," he said, as the trolley laden with documents was parked immediately next to me, "that the debt remains. In case you were, against all expectation, to win the lottery . . ." He gave me a wry smile.

"But for the time being . . ."

149

He leaned forward even further. I could feel his breath. A faint smell of curry and gastric acid. He stroked his chin with one finger, as if he still hadn't quite made up his mind.

". . . we won't make any efforts to call it in. It will simply be frozen. Do you understand?"

I said nothing.

Pierre went on, "Are we in agreement?"

I glanced at Maud, but she was sitting there straight-backed, writing something down, so I turned back to Pierre. I could see a trace of sweat on his top lip, shimmering in the glow of the fluorescent lighting. I noticed that Maud had started to gather her papers together, and she might have brushed against me briefly under the table as she leaned over to put some documents back in her briefcase. I'm not entirely sure.

"Does this mean . . .?" I began.

All three men were looking at me now, and I could feel Maud tense up next to me. It was as if they were suddenly all worried that I was about to throw a spanner in the works. The two foreign gentlemen straightened up.

"Does this mean that I can carry on with my life more or less as before?" I said.

Pierre looked at me unhappily. Then he slowly nodded.

"If you could just . . ." he said, passing me a pen. "If you could just sign this. On each page. You understand, this must remain utterly confidential."

I looked down at the first sheet of paper.

CHAPTER
TWENTY-FOUR

Down at the ice-cream kiosk that evening I caught sight of the girl with the necklaces again, the one I recognised from the reception desk and whose phone call I had overheard in the lift. She was walking quickly away from the bus. She looked harassed, frowning deeply as she passed by in a hurry. She didn't buy an ice-cream. Maybe she was having to save money?

It was a magical evening, the air clear after the heavy rain. The sky, trees and people were all reflected in little puddles that were gradually drying in the mild evening sunlight. It was as if everything had been given a fresh start.

My phone buzzed in my pocket. I pulled it out and looked at the screen. Roger. I wondered if he'd sold his boat. He only let it ring once, then he hung up. He did this a couple of times, then a text arrived.

Call me!

I realised that it was urgent. This was the second time in a week that he had gone to the expense of sending a text. I'm not sure I'd ever received a text from Roger before that. Apart from the time he was on a course in personal development and I suddenly received a message out of the blue, saying, *I find you attractive, exciting, and I think of you as a very good friend. Fondest wishes, Roger.* Roger's brother, Eric, had booked and paid in advance to attend the course himself, but at the last minute was unable to go. Food and lodging were included, which is why Roger agreed to go in his place. The tender message turned out to be the last part of an exercise in showing your appreciation of other people. It was some sort of group message sent free of charge from one of the course computers. "I had to adapt it slightly so it would work for everyone," he said afterwards when I asked what he had meant by "attractive".

I called him and he answered on the first ring.

"Listen," he said, "I've had one of those forms now."

"What forms?" I said.

"From W. R. D.," he said. "Obviously I appealed against the amount. And now I've finally got them to agree to look at my case again. And I've got one of their forms to fill in any 'gaps' or 'blank periods', or whatever the hell they call them. Presumably they've got things missing from their records that you have to give them information about . . ."

"Okay," I said.

"You have to tell them who you saw on certain days, and so on. Then I suppose they double-check against the records of the people you mention."

I pulled on my jacket. Not because it was cold, but because I wanted to look a bit smarter. Among the receipts and old sweets in the pocket I found a new

152

scrap of paper. I pulled it out and saw that it contained a phone number and a name. *Maud*, it said. I looked at the number and saw that it was different to the one I had called before. A mobile number.

"Well," Roger said, "I thought I'd give them your name."

I ran my thumb over the numbers on the piece of paper. She had written them very neatly. Her handwriting leaned forward slightly, and looked rather ornate and old-fashioned.

"What did you say?" I said.

"I just thought it was simpler that way. And you don't have to come up with anything. You just have to say yes if they ask you."

I folded the piece of paper with Maud's number on it and tucked it into my inside pocket instead. A ball came rolling towards me, and a small boy ran after it. I stopped the ball with my foot and the boy picked it up without looking at me.

"Hang on," I said. "What did you say?"

"Look, I'm not so stupid that I didn't realise they give you loads of points the more people you mention, and the more fun you say you've had. So I thought that . . . Well, I thought I'd give your name, for everything."

I didn't reply at first.

"Hello? *Hello?* Are you still there?" Roger shouted down the phone.

"Look . . ." I said hesitantly. "I don't think . . . No."

He was panting the way he usually did, and I wondered if he was on his way somewhere.

"There's nothing funny about it," he said. "If they call and ask, you just have to say: Yes, I was with Roger. That's all."

"No," I said. "I don't think that's such a good idea."

"What? Why not?" He let out a sigh. "Look, it's not like you'd have to lie. You'd just have to . . . confirm what I say."

"No," I said.

"God, you're really touchy all of a sudden. I mean, we *have* met, haven't we? And I can't list everyone else I've . . . Hang on, are you ashamed of me or something?"

"Of course I'm not," I said. "I just think . . . How can I put it? This business of us spending time together . . . well, it might increase your score."

He was quiet for a few seconds. I could hear him breathing through his nose.

"What do you mean by that?" he eventually said.

"Oh, I just think . . . Look, can't you try to remember what really happened instead?"

He snorted.

"Are you worried about your own score going up? Because you've spent time with me? But it's true, though, isn't it? We do know each other. Don't we? Or are you denying that?"

"No," I said. "Of course I'm not. I just mean . . ."

"Ah!" Roger said, as if he'd suddenly worked out what I was thinking. "You think you're going to end up with a much higher score if they find out you've been spending a lot of time with me. That's what it is, isn't it?"

"No, that's not what I think . . ."

"It is! Admit it!"

"Please, Roger, just . . ."

"What?" he said impatiently.

"Just don't do it!" I said.

He said nothing for a while, as if he was thinking. He sighed.

"I'm going to," he said. "I can't keep making allowances for you the whole damn time. I'm sorry."

"But surely you could . . . Maybe you could say we mostly speak on the phone?" I said.

"What's wrong with you?" Roger yelled. "Christ, you could at least try to help me out once in a while."

The ball came back again, followed by the boy, but this time it was too far away for me to be able to stop it. It came to a halt with a splash in one of the puddles.

"Okay, okay," I said. "Do as you like."

We hung up without me finding out what had happened to his boat.

I took out the piece of paper with Maud's number. I ran my fingers over the numbers again before putting it back in the pocket I had first found it in. I tried to work out if I dare ask her round to mine. Was that allowed? Would she dare to take the risk? How would that affect her career? But she herself had said that only things that had happened up to now counted. And the men in the meeting had indicated that I could carry on with my life as though nothing had happened.

I wandered slowly and aimlessly through the city, looking at the people around me. Young people, middle-aged people. A little girl rode past me on a big, red woman's bicycle. Somewhere a radio was playing "Clouds" by Frank Sinatra. A flock of birds was wheeling through the air like a single entity. Did they do that, I wondered, to pretend that they're bigger than they are to predators, or so that a predator wouldn't be able to target a particular individual?

I looked at all the familiar things in my life. The buildings, streets, trees. The ice-cream kiosk and shops. The lunchtime crowds in restaurants. The posters on the walls and the newspaper flysheets. My fingers toyed with the note in my pocket. Of all the people around me, only I knew that I was probably the happiest person in the country. And at absolutely no cost. I took a deep breath of the mild summer air. It occurred to me that I could have some ice-cream. Mint chocolate and raspberry, my two favourites.

Other titles published by Ulverscroft:

THE ROOM

Jonas Karlsson

The Authority looks favourably upon meticulousness, efficiency and ambition. Bjorn has all of this in spades, but it's only in the room that he can really shine. And it's only in the room that he finds harmony, an escape from the triviality of the workplace. Unfortunately, his colleagues see things differently. In fact, they don't appear to see the room at all — eventually leaving Bjorn convinced that they are conducting some sort of psychological warfare against him. But who is right? Is the room a figment of an overactive imagination, the spectre of a mental illness? Or is there something more mysterious going on?

SMILE

Roddy Doyle

Just moved in to a new apartment, alone for the first time in years, Victor Forde goes every evening to Donnelly's pub for a pint. One evening a man in shorts and a pink shirt brings over his own pint and sits down. He seems to know Victor's name and to remember him from school. Says his name is Fitzpatrick. Victor dislikes him on sight; dislikes the memories that Fitzpatrick stirs up of five years being taught by the Christian Brothers. He prompts other recollections too — of Rachel, his beautiful wife who became a celebrity, and of Victor's small claim to fame as the man who says the unsayable on the radio. But it's the memories of school, and of one particular Brother, that he cannot control, and which eventually threaten to destroy his sanity . . .